A LADY TO LEAD

BOOKS BY AUDREY GLENN

Sweet Historical Romance with Diana Davis

A Gentleman's Daughter

A Lady to Lead

Freedom's Ring

Revolution's Call

Be sure to join Audrey's mailing list to be the first to know about her new releases! Also get fun bonuses from this book, book recommendations, freebies and more!

http://love.DiDavisAuthor.com/newsletter2

A LADY TO LEAD

SISTERS
of the
REVOLUTION #2

Audrey Glenn

DCB

DAUGHTERS OF COLUMBIA BOOKS

First printing, 2020

Published by Daughters of Columbia Books

ISBN 978-1-940096-42-1

PRINTED IN THE UNITED STATES OF AMERICA

—For Cliff
This is a business trip!

Chapter 1

Helen Crofton readjusted her tan and floral jacket for the third time and made absolutely no difference to her appearance. The jacket was fine—it was Helen that was discomfited. In another hour, her sister Cassandra would nominate her as president of their charitable society, and they could finally do some good. Or something at all.

If the other young ladies accepted her, that was. At least her dark hair looked well—powdered and curled in the latest fashion. She'd been practicing looking friendly as well.

Helen closed the door to her bedroom and followed her brother-in-law's voice to the drawing room, recently repainted in the gray-blue color he favored.

David Beaufort stood back to admire the lines on his latest acquisition. "What a remarkably elegant chair."

"Was it worth the time you spent deliberating, dearest?" Cassandra asked. Her tone carried a note of teasing, as if they hadn't been subjected to David's agonizing for weeks.

"Don't you think so? You can sit turned any way you like."

He sat to demonstrate, pivoting from right to left while leaning against each side of the backrest in turn. "Perfect for parties. I can speak to your aunt and then turn to Dr. Rush with no discomfort at all!"

"Hmm," Cassandra said. She massaged her lower back.

"Oh—you should sit, my love." David sprang from the seat and beckoned to his pregnant wife to take his place, helping her into the chair.

"Are you ready?" Helen interrupted, stepping farther into the drawing room.

David whirled around. "Ah, Helen! You should have a turn also!"

His smile was infectious. "It's a lovely chair," Helen conceded. "Perhaps I can try it later."

"Do you want to leave now?" Cassandra asked.

"I don't want to risk being late," she explained.

"Leaving so soon? Let me send Westing down to the stables to order our coach." David started for the door immediately.

"No need," Cassandra called out before he could leave. "We can walk down and order the coach ourselves."

"Westing doesn't mind going." David turned back. "He could use the fresh air."

"As can we." Cassandra used the arm of the new chair to push herself up. David rushed back to help her the rest of the way to her feet.

Helen eyed the clock on the mantel.

"Don't forget to order the coach," David admonished. "I don't want anything to happen to you or the baby. It's a long walk to the Hayeses' home."

"We'll be perfectly safe for the entire mile, I assure you! Now, what will you do while we're gone?"

David sat in his new chair again. "Visit the coffee room

and then collect Nathaniel for dinner."

This caught Helen's attention. "Captain Carter?" she groaned. "Is he to dine with us?"

"I told David he could invite a friend," Cassandra explained.

"I thought Captain Carter was a business associate."

"I like him, and it *is* my birthday," David pointed out.

"You couldn't think of anyone else in Philadelphia to invite? What about Dr. Rush?"

David opened his mouth to respond, probably something about how Helen didn't care for Dr. Rush either, but Cassandra used one finger to lift his chin. She leaned down to kiss her husband, and Helen glanced away for decency's sake.

"Are you sure you don't want me to escort you?" David asked, and Helen knew it was safe to look again.

"Certainly not. Enjoy the coffee room. And your chair."

"Be careful, please, dearest." David kissed Cassandra's hand then looked to Helen. "Good luck today."

Helen nodded. "Oh—thank you." Luck would be irrelevant if they were late.

"Come," Cassandra said. Fastening their cloaks, they made their way down the narrow stairs from the second-floor apartment over their uncle's law office. Helen didn't see Uncle Josiah among his clerks to bid him goodbye. Perhaps he was in his private study or in court.

The ladies began for their aunt and uncle's home in the chilly October air. In front of the stable where their coach and horses were housed, Helen took care to walk around a pile of horse droppings. Cassandra walked past the stable without stopping. "Didn't you tell David we would ask for the coach?" Helen asked.

"I told him we *could* order it. I didn't say we *would*."

Helen laughed. "Very clever misdirection." Cassandra was

determined not to be wrapped away in linen until after the baby came.

"You needn't race there," Cassandra chided. "We're quite early."

"I'm sorry. I just don't want to be late." Helen forced herself to walk at what felt like a snail's pace.

"All will be well," Cassandra assured her. "I'll nominate you as president, and I'm certain Patience or Constance will second it."

"But will they vote for me, or will they all wish to see Temperance reelected instead?"

Cassandra looped her arm through Helen's. "I doubt Temperance wants to be president again. She seemed to lose interest very quickly."

"You're too polite to say we accomplished *nothing* under her tenure! Temperance wasted every meeting talking of balls and beaus. How can we even call ourselves a charitable society?" Helen scowled at the memory.

"Spending an hour in conversation with our friends is not completely wasted time," her sister pointed out.

"*Your* friends," Helen said in an undertone. "I don't think any of them like me."

Cassandra shook her head. "We've talked about this. They *do* like you."

"Then why did no one support my ideas? I suggested we hold a subscription ball to raise money for a statue of William Penn—"

"—which Patience rightly pointed out would not be sufficiently profitable," Cassandra interrupted.

"I also suggested we beautify the grounds surrounding the potter's field in North Square."

"Even *you* didn't want to dig about in the dirt."

"Well, we did absolutely nothing to improve the city or

help its residents. I can't bear to listen to Temperance describe her dance partners and wardrobe every week for another year. I'm determined that this year we'll do *something*."

"We shall," Cassandra reassured her. "The other ladies might feel the same way. You should encourage everyone to speak up with her thoughts on what we could do."

"If they had any ideas, they would have spoken up by now," Helen retorted. She supported Cassandra over a crack in the road.

"Not everyone has your ability to express themselves openly. Try to listen to the other ladies before pushing ahead with your own ideas."

Helen was silent for a moment, considering her sister's words. "I think a great deal about my ideas before I present them. Are they really terrible?"

"No! You have wonderful ideas! I'm only asking you to listen to the other ladies, not stay entirely silent."

"I'll try," Helen conceded. "Though I won't settle on a terrible plan for the society in the name of harmony. If I'm even elected president," she added as an afterthought.

Despite Cassandra's leisurely speed, they arrived at the Hayeses' brick home plenty early for the meeting. Ginny, a maid, answered the door.

"How is your mother?" Helen asked, handing over her cloak to Ginny.

"Dr. Drinker's been by to see her. Says her heart is weak."

"Oh dear, perhaps we can visit her soon," Cassandra offered.

"Thank you; she would like that." Ginny curtsied before leading them in.

Helen couldn't resist smirking at her sister. Dr. Drinker had been very pointed in his attentions to Cassandra before she married David. Cassandra blushed and wouldn't meet her eyes. She always insisted the relationship was strictly professional.

Their cousin Patience Hayes sat at a table in the elegant, green-paneled drawing room, scribbling away. She glanced up when they walked in and smiled politely before returning to her work. "Is it time already? Temperance should be down soon. I have to finish this volume of Virginia legal cases for Papa's trial. I've managed to find one instance where a general court prevented a magistrate from setting aside a jury's verdict, but I'd like to find a few more."

"Your father is very fortunate to have your assistance," Helen said, taking a seat on the couch next to Patience.

Patience shook her head wryly. "With no sons, he has no other options. He says most of his current clerks don't have much promise."

"You would be an asset if he had half a dozen sons." As a child, Helen had often sat in her own father's lap while he spoke to his steward. Sometimes he would ask her opinions. How adult and respected he'd made her feel! Patience was blessed to have a father who trusted her to do research for him.

Jane Allen arrived next, dressed in a simple gray gown befitting her father's Quaker faith. She quietly took her seat.

Helen's stomach churned. Not much longer now and she'd find out if she would be in a position to make changes in the society.

Temperance Hayes glided into the drawing room, her sister Constance trailing behind. Helen had often wished to have a small portion of her cousins' dazzling beauty.

"Are we all here?" Temperance took a chair prominently placed near the fire. "I'll ring for tea."

Euphemia Goodwin burst into the room. "I'm ever so

sorry: my dancing master kept me so long! Am I late?"

"Not at all," Helen reassured Euphemia, who took her seat as well.

"Put that book away, Constance," Temperance admonished her sister. "I have an announcement."

Constance dutifully stuffed a novel behind her back and looked expectantly towards Temperance.

"I want you all to know that I shan't run for reelection as president. I'll be unable to devote the time required, as I shall soon enter a different sphere of life."

Patience's lips tightened.

"Whatever do you mean?" Euphemia asked, eyes wide.

Temperance toyed with a lock of hair. "I can say no more. Nothing is yet official."

"She plans to be married," Constance whispered loudly.

Euphemia squealed and clapped. "How wonderful! Who is the man?"

Temperance lowered her voice. "As I said, nothing is official, and it would be extremely improper of me to say more. I just wanted all of you to know that the *only* thing that could possibly prevent me from carrying on with the noble work of this society is an even higher calling. I'm certain I can trust each of you not to spread this about before it's settled." Temperance sat back in her chair and folded her hands in her lap like royalty.

Temperance must have finally captured Winthrop Morley's attentions. She'd been angling to marry the governor's worthless scoundrel of a son for as long as the sisters had known her.

"Should we call for nominations for a new president?" Patience suggested.

"I nominate Helen," Cassandra said quickly. Helen observed the other ladies' reactions. Jane was grave as always, while Constance nodded slowly. Temperance seemed surprised, but Patience smiled approvingly.

"How wonderful!" Euphemia declared. "I second the nomination!"

Helen beamed at her. She hadn't expected support from that quarter, but she vowed she would never again be annoyed with Euphemia's prattle.

"Anyone else?" Patience asked. Helen reminded herself to breathe.

No one suggested another name.

"All in favor?"

All hands raised. Helen looked around the room at the other ladies and her heart swelled.

"Very good; the 'ayes' have it. Helen, you are our new president."

Helen stood hastily and shook out her petticoat. She tried to remember what she'd planned to say if actually elected. "Thank you for your trust in me. I hope I shall honor this society by my efforts. I'd especially like to choose a charitable project we could begin immediately."

Euphemia hung off her chair and frantically waved one hand in the air, dainty mouth pursed with excitement. "I just know you'll do an admirable job, Helen, and I'm delighted to join all of you in this righteous endeavor. I think there's a great deal wrong with this city that we young ladies can set to rights, for it's not just the gentlemen of Philadelphia who are able to enact reforms. In fact, I was just saying to my father—"

"Thank you, Euphemia," Helen said quickly. Euphemia was unlikely to stop talking without help. "Perhaps you can tell us what you said to your father after the meeting."

Euphemia threw her hands over her face. "I'm sorry," she apologized, her words muffled.

Helen smiled politely at her. "Are there any ideas for

projects?"

"We could knit caps for the poor," Constance suggested. "It must be very troublesome to be poor when it is this cold."

Helen didn't want to admit in front of the accomplished Hayes sisters that neither she nor her sister could knit.

"That's certainly one idea," Helen said, mindful of her sister's advice not to force only her own ideas. "Any others?"

Jane raised a hand. "I've become aware of a young girl, just fifteen, who arrived from England in the spring. She has become the recipient of some very improper attentions from her master's son, which have made her very unhappy, but her contract is in force for six more years."

Helen's breath caught. She'd very nearly been sold into indenture with her sister when they'd first arrived in Philadelphia. How many nights had she laid awake trying not to imagine what could have happened to them if their uncle hadn't arrived in time to rescue them?

"I feel for her most intensely!" Temperance declared. "This must be our project."

Helen tried not to let her impatience show. Temperance had had her chance to help others when she was president, and Helen had respected her position. She deserved the same.

"We'll put it to a vote," Helen announced. To her relief, this motion also passed unanimously.

"How can we raise money for the contract?" Patience asked. "Indentures for a young person can cost as much as twenty-five pounds."

"I'll ask my father to give us the money!" Euphemia offered.

"I think, perhaps, we should raise the money ourselves," Helen replied. "It won't be truly our work if we ask the men in our lives to pay for it."

"Oh," Euphemia sighed. "Twenty pounds is such a sizable

sum! But—oh! We might each sell our hair! My maid told me that a really fine head might garner five pounds, and there are seven of us here—we might almost free two servants!"

Helen wasn't the only lady to automatically raise a hand in protection of her hair. She was proud of her abundant brown tresses—perhaps a pious person might say *too* proud. Surely there was another way.

"Very admirable sentiment," she managed. "Any other ideas?"

"We could sell a baked good in the city market," Jane suggested.

"Oh, yes!" Helen said. "Our father used to host a fête every year to benefit our poorest tenants, and Cassandra and I always contributed to the baked goods sale."

Euphemia clapped with excitement. "We should make a syllabub. I love syllabub above all things!"

"That might be very difficult, Euphemia," Jane pointed out. "A syllabub must be consumed just when it is made, and one could not prepare very many at once."

"Gooseberry tarts!" The words burst from Helen's mouth. "They were always very popular and sold for a great deal." Happy memories flooded her mind. She hadn't fully appreciated how wonderful her life had been until her parents died and everything changed.

Patience frowned. "Gooseberries aren't in season."

"We can use gooseberry preserves," Helen countered. Gooseberry tarts would certainly prove just as profitable to sell in Philadelphia as they had at Heartcomb.

"I thought we might serve gingerbread," Jane said. "It's easy to cut and stays fresh for several days when wrapped."

"We dined on gooseberry tart at the governor's house this summer," Helen pointed out. "And Mrs. Morley is very fashionable and elite."

Jane nodded, though the set to her lips made her appear less than convinced.

"It's settled then," Helen announced. "I'll draw up a plan for the entire scheme, and we'll discuss it at our next meeting. This meeting is adjourned."

After visiting a while, the sisters took their leave. The day was crisp and clear, and the last of the autumn leaves provided a lovely frame for the beautiful red-brick city.

Helen slid her arm through her sister's. "I love this city in the fall!"

"Well, sister dear, were you pleased with the meeting?" Cassandra asked.

"Yes, I think it went very well. That young girl we are to help—that could have easily been you and me."

"Thank heaven for our uncle!" Cassandra paused to wave to one of David's business associates across the street. As they neared their apartment in the center of town, Pine Street grew more crowded with people and horses.

"I can't wait to make the gooseberry tarts. It will feel like home again!" Helen's mouth watered. She could almost taste the tart berries.

"Are you certain you know how to make them? As I recall, we didn't really do much more than watch Cook prepare the tarts."

"I remember every detail," Helen insisted. "And I've Mama's household book to refer to."

"Receipts are often more difficult to execute than to read," Cassandra pointed out. "Perhaps Peggy knows how to make them."

Helen patted her sister's hand. "I'm certain I can manage, but if I can't, I'll ask our cook for assistance." Peggy was expert at everything in the kitchen. She surely had something excellent planned for David's birthday dinner. Helen suddenly recalled the guest list. "Why didn't you tell me Captain Carter was coming for dinner?"

Cassandra chuckled. "Perhaps I didn't wish to hear you complain of it for days!"

"I wouldn't have," Helen protested. "It's just that he's extremely disagreeable. Do you not recall how rude he was to me at your wedding? First, he ignored me, then he laid hands upon my person—"

"To try to save your life, if I remember," her sister interjected.

"—refused to laugh about the whole thing, and treated me like a spectacle at a village fair," Helen finished.

Cassandra huffed. "That was nearly three years ago! Can't you find it in your heart to forgive him and try to be civil?"

"I *always* attempt to make conversation with him *every* time his company is forced upon me. The last time I saw him I asked him about his new ship, and he answered in three words. Then he turned to David and spoke at length of the Pennsylvania silk industry."

"An excessively boring discussion," Cassandra had to own. "He may be a dull man, but he's not a bad one. Please be patient with him, for David's sake—he seems to genuinely like Captain Carter."

Helen didn't want to promise too much with respect to the captain, so she changed the subject. "I hope I'll have sufficient time to change my gown."

"What a kind idea—that will please David."

Helen grinned. "I doubt he'll be pleased when he sees me in my old gray mourning dress."

"Helen, you mustn't!" Cassandra protested. "Wear that nice pink silk gown David bought you."

"It would probably be churlish of me not to," Helen conceded, "though it will be wasted on Captain Carter."

This dinner must be endured, but as early as she could politely manage, she would escape to her bedroom and begin working on the plan for the society.

Chapter 2

Nathaniel Carter groaned and threw a crumpled note across the room. This wasn't the news he needed today.

"Hold!"

Nathaniel looked up to see David Beaufort, one of his most important investors, standing in the doorway.

"I surrender!" David scooped the paper up from the floor and tossed it back at Nathaniel. David was, as always, impeccably dressed in a blue coat he probably considered plain, though it was toggled and braided, and his waistcoat was covered in embroidery.

Nathaniel caught the ball of paper easily and tried to smooth it out before tossing it down on the desk. "Did you hear?" He waved to the paper. "He had that fool son of his deliver a letter personally." He didn't attempt to hide his contempt, and David's grimace concurred. Winthrop Morley was one of the most insufferable men he'd ever met. David's father was a marquess—far above a provincial governor—and *he'd* never asked Nathaniel to bow and scrape. Winthrop was content to throw his father's name around and let better men do all the hard work.

David's eyes raked over the page on Nathaniel's desk. "I heard rumors in the coffee room this morning. Governor Morley can't possibly stop all contraband tea from coming into Philadelphia."

"He intends to," Nathaniel growled. "This newfound loyalty he's mustered to king and country is surprising. He's been turning a blind eye to smuggling for the last decade."

David snorted. "I hear the custom houses have promised the governor a cut of all the East India Company tea sold at market. By keeping smuggled tea out, he ensures high demand for the legal variety."

Nathaniel slapped his desk. "I knew there was something in it for him!"

David helped himself to the chair in front of Nathaniel's desk, having learned long since that Nathaniel had no inclination for social niceties. Nathaniel's office, a tiny room at the back of his warehouse, would be considered snug by most. To a man who had lived aboard ships his entire life the room seemed nearly palatial, possessing a desk, two chairs, a large framed map of the known world, and a lantern for working late nights.

"When that load of madeira sells you must purchase yourself better chairs with the profits." David wrinkled his nose in distaste as he examined the unornamented wooden arms of his seat.

Nathaniel didn't mind hard chairs. He'd never been softened by the luxuries David insisted on. "The *Raleigh* departed only a month ago. We'll not see her return before next year, and by that time, I may need the profit to recover my losses from this tea catastrophe." Nathaniel sighed heavily and leaned back in his chair, which really wasn't very comfortable, if he was honest with himself.

"What do you mean to do?"

"I must bring the tea to market despite the governor's interference." Nathaniel rubbed his forehead.

"You must not involve yourself in anything unlawful," David admonished. "Smugglers are subject to a hefty fine, not to mention the loss of all the smuggled goods."

Nathaniel shot David a hard look. "Nine out of every ten cases of tea in this city have been brought in unlawfully. You've had no problem with my smuggling before now."

David shrugged. "That was before the governor decided he cared! Smuggling didn't really seem like a crime before. You'll have to find something else to do with it."

"There's nothing else to do with it. The Southern colonies will not purchase what they deem 'inferior' Dutch tea. Boston and New York already have established supply lines, and their markets cannot easily bear more."

"Store it in New Jersey?" David suggested.

"Too expensive, and everyone will think of that. In a month or two, when all the merchants in this town grow desperate enough, each will try to smuggle it in at once and the market will be flooded with tea. If we want to turn a profit, or just avoid a total loss, we must act now."

"You could just pay the taxes."

"We'd record a loss." Nathaniel groaned and placed his head in his hands.

David got to his feet. "Well, I've trusted you thus far, and you have amply repaid me. Are you changing before dinner?"

Nathaniel looked up. "About that—I think it would be best if I stayed here and worked on a plan to bring the tea in without interference."

"I don't suppose every merchant in Philadelphia will

determine how to overtake you if you allow yourself one afternoon to celebrate the birthday of your greatest investor!" David retorted.

Nathaniel wasn't sure what to say. He didn't want to offend such an important financial backer, but he did not relish spending an afternoon in awkward and forced conversation. David's wife was pleasant enough, but his sister-in-law was a termagant.

He couldn't fathom why Helen seemed to dislike him so much; he'd been nothing but courteous to her each time they met. He'd even saved her life once by thumping her on the back when she was choking on a piece of cake. Lately he'd taken to trying to speak to her as little as possible so as not to draw her ire.

Even knowing he probably wasn't escaping the dinner, Nathaniel made one final attempt. "I'm sure you could celebrate adequately without me."

"A single man like yourself should jump at the chance to dine with a beautiful young lady."

A suspicion crossed Nathaniel's mind. "You're not attempting to foist her off on me, are you?"

David appeared to consider the idea seriously. "It would save me a great deal in housing and feeding her, not to mention her clothing. Excellent idea."

"I've no need of a wife," Nathaniel insisted. "My time is spent on my work."

"A wife could make your life more comfortable."

"I can't see how!" Nathaniel protested. "I've everything I need without one. I eat my dinner at the tavern; I pay a woman to launder my clothing. I mend my own tack, and I don't entertain guests. A wife would be far more costly than what I would get in return."

"That's one way to see things," David said solemnly,

though there was laughter in his eyes. "No need to worry; I'm not ready to throw my sister-in-law away on just anyone. I have a whole series of tests planned for any likely candidates." David rubbed his hands together, evidently relishing the prospect.

While he was speaking, Nathaniel slid into his black coat, plain compared to David's.

"I gather you won't change your clothing. Very well, follow me to my home."

They stepped out of the warehouse, David waiting so Nathaniel could lock the door behind him. He would have to find another place to store the contraband tea, as this location was the first place the governor would search.

Door secured, the two men set out. Nathaniel liked the red-bricked city—especially the smooth, cobbled roads. They made carrying cargo from the docks to the warehouse much easier.

David wrinkled his nose distastefully. "I'll never grow accustomed to this odor," he complained. The fish market was winding down for the day, but the smell lingered in the air.

"They didn't have odors in England, of course," Nathaniel teased.

"I am certain they must have, but I was never forced to endure them!"

David lived only a few streets away, near the Pennsylvania State House. The men entered the brick row building and bypassed the lawyer's office to the left, now dark, opting for the narrow stairs on the right.

"Wait in there while I go find my wife," David said, motioning to the drawing room.

Nathaniel dutifully entered the room and nearly turned around to walk out again. Helen Crofton was standing at the fireplace, back turned to him.

Nathaniel considered where he might go. Back to stand in the antechamber? He was not familiar with the rest of the apartment.

Helen didn't bother to hide her disappointment when she turned and caught sight of him. She dipped into the barest of curtsies. "Do you wish to sit?"

"Thank you." Nathaniel settled in a corner chair he'd not seen on previous visits. Helen settled onto the couch and arranged her skirt. Every time he saw her, he was reminded that she was very pretty—not that it held any weight with him. Had the pink silk of her gown been made in Pennsylvania? It was very becoming. Perhaps there was something to American silk after all.

They sat in silence for some minutes, long enough that it became amusing to Nathaniel to imagine who would speak first.

"Do you care to explain your smile, Captain?"

"I'm not currently the captain of a vessel," he corrected.

She glanced at the mantel clock. "I thought once a captain, always a captain," she retorted.

He shook his head but didn't elaborate. Helen raised her eyebrows. Did she expect him to raise another topic of conversation? He wasn't sure what courtesy demanded.

"Captain Carter! Thank you for coming to celebrate my husband's birthday." Nathaniel was relieved by Cassandra's rescue. At least someone was happy to see him.

"The pleasure is all mine, I assure you." He bowed over her hand. She wore a blue silk only a few shades darker than the color of the living room walls. He supposed David favored the color.

David stepped into the room after her. "Ah! Do you like my new chair? It's a Chippendale."

Nathaniel hadn't noticed anything special about it. "Very

nice."

"I believe dinner is laid out if you care to follow me?" David had changed into a white coat embroidered with a gold scroll pattern and a very expensive-looking wig. Maybe Nathaniel should have changed his coat.

He wondered if he ought to offer Helen his arm, but she stepped past him without glancing his way, so he was left to trail after her. Her scent wafted in the air as they stepped down the corridor to the dining room; Nathaniel found the lemony smell very appropriate for her sour disposition.

Nathaniel found he could do great service to the meal laid before him despite the fact that he'd tried to get out of attending. The family kept an excellent cook. David's valet, Westing, hovered in the corner watching for any chance to be of service to the family.

Cassandra attempted to make conversation with Nathaniel by inquiring about his three merchant ships.

Helen tried to seem concerned. "Any chance of leaving on a prolonged voyage?" David and Cassandra exchanged a look.

"Now that I own three ships, I must coordinate the business of all, and I can't do that separated from the post for months at a time." He could remain civil despite Helen's obvious rudeness.

Cassandra spoke before Helen could. "Do you miss sailing?"

Nathaniel considered the question. "I miss the order of my ship, and always knowing exactly what I must do next. I don't miss the hard tack. This is far more to my taste." He held up a fresh roll. Westing seemed to take it as a sign he wanted more bread and rushed to offer more.

"How was the Young Society Ladies Meeting?" David inquired, turning to Helen.

"Philadelphia Young Ladies Charitable Society," Helen corrected. "It was excellent!" We've agreed to buy out the indenture of a young lady who is in a very desperate circumstance."

"I suppose that means I should expect to be asked to make a donation?"

"No!" Helen protested. "We young ladies mean to earn all the money ourselves, for it is certainly not just gentlemen who can find success in business."

"We mean to sell gooseberry tarts at the city market," Cassandra explained. "Helen is in charge of the entire scheme. She was elected president today!"

David approved. "Excellent! Gooseberries are very fashionable."

"Just what I said!" Helen beamed at David.

"An indenture is quite dear," Nathaniel could not help saying. He wasn't in the habit of purchasing desserts, but they couldn't be very expensive. He started to do some calculations in his mind. "You must mean to sell a great quantity of pies."

"Tarts," Helen corrected stiffly. "I've not precisely calculated how many we must sell, but I'm certain we can manage it. Our friends and families will buy many tarts, and the market is always crowded."

"A market stall can be very expensive to rent," Nathaniel pointed out.

Helen shrugged. "We'll have to raise the money for the stall somehow."

He persisted. "Where will you get the gooseberries? I don't know much about fruits, but I can't imagine they are in season."

"We'll use preserves. I thank you for your help, but I'm certain we're capable of managing everything without assistance."

Why was she so averse to a bit of advice from someone far more experienced in business matters? Nathaniel thrived on sound advice when he was starting out.

"You'll need to learn from someone," David interjected. "Young ladies aren't exactly in the habit of running a business. Perhaps you *should* ask for donations."

Nathaniel agreed. "I will pledge five pence to you," he offered.

"I should not take a ha'penny off you!" Helen clenched her fork.

Nathaniel was taken aback. He'd only been trying to help.

"I attended a meeting today," David interjected. "Of a private organization that wants to free the colonies from unfair taxation."

Helen scoffed. "We all know you speak of the Sons of Liberty!"

David narrowed his eyes. "This *private* organization means to host an assembly to determine what to do about the Tea Act which Parliament saw fit to pass."

Nathaniel wasn't impressed. "I know of the Sons of Liberty, and I would not trust a one of them to keep his word, not after what happened in Boston a few years ago."

"That was unfortunate," David admitted. "Though most of the merchants did stick to the agreement not to import the English goods."

Nathaniel took a sip of wine. "I won't be making any decisions based on the paper promises of that lot. You were still in England then."

"I think most of them are very sincere, and only a handful of merchants went back on their word. Most of the Sons of Liberty believe in promoting freedom."

"Aye—freedom for themselves, to make as much money as they can," Nathaniel replied. "Though perhaps that's the noblest cause of all."

Helen watched the debate closely. "You don't seem to believe anyone can accomplish anything! You must have had a very sad upbringing. Were you orphaned as a small child?"

Cassandra blanched. "Helen!"

"No," Nathaniel refuted. "I had a perfectly normal boyhood with a mother and father." He didn't add that his father died when Nathaniel was only seven, or that his mother had given him to his uncle to employ on a ship shortly after so she could marry a local widower. It hadn't been detrimental to his development at all.

Helen only sniffed and stayed silent for the rest of the meal.

After dinner, Nathaniel declined to stay for champagne or coffee. "I've plans to develop," he said by way of an excuse.

David walked him out to the street. "I thank you for coming. Will you shake hands with me, or have I done you too great a mischief by forcing you to endure Helen's company?"

"I will shake, and gladly. No harm was done to me."

"I don't know why you bring out the worst in Helen. She's really a pleasant companion most of the time."

"All the better she remains in your household," Nathaniel joked, and he took his leave. A sound made him turn back when he was only a little way down the street. Helen was looking out a window, glaring at him as if he were her bitterest enemy. It didn't seem to matter how hard he tried to help; she was displeased by everything he said.

He laughed, crammed his hands into his pockets, and made his way down the street. Helen Crofton's opinions didn't matter to him in the least. He turned his thoughts towards what he would have to do to get his illegal shipment of tea into the city.

Chapter 3

Helen looked over the long line of market stalls. She and Constance had inquired about space to rent at nearly every stall in the most fashionable row at the market. Helen thought it would be best to stay near the other bakers and fine jewelers rather than setting up a blanket by the rag pickers bordering the main building, but they were running out of options.

"Let's try this one," Helen suggested. She walked right up to the baker, Constance trailing a few steps behind.

"Would you rent me space in your stall?" Helen asked boldly. She was too tired to mince words.

"What are you selling?" The baker, a stout man with a square jaw, scrutinized her.

"Tarts." The man gave her a once-over. "Gooseberry tarts," Helen quickly amended. "For charity." Explaining what the ladies planned to do with their earnings had turned out to be a bad idea, as many of the merchants who sold in this market held indenture contracts and wouldn't tolerate a hint of liberation talk.

"Ten shillings a week, and you can use that." The baker shoved a finger to a rough wooden table behind them.

"Thank you, but that's more money than we have to spend. Come, Constance." Helen grabbed her cousin's elbow and gently steered her out into the main thoroughfare of the market. It was crowded on a workday morning with everyone from servants to fashionable ladies attempting to complete their shopping.

Two pounds a month was the lowest offer they'd heard, but it was still far more than all the money in the society's treasury.

"Do you not think it would be the most romantic thing in the world for two people to meet at a bakery stall and fall in love?" Constance asked, absorbed in some fantasy.

"I'm afraid I fail to see the romance in that," Helen admitted. Constance was always half-in, half-out of a day-dream on account of Aunt Anne allowing her daughters to read so many sentimental novels. Helen's own governess had never permitted such vain pursuits.

Helen would have preferred Cassandra's company, but her sister had promised to spend the morning returning calls with David. Constance might not be much practical use, but Helen liked her dreamy cousin, and she didn't really need someone to take over. She'd spent hours perfecting the tart plan. Even Captain Carter couldn't find fault with her now! He seemed to think that just because she was a woman, she was completely ignorant and would be grateful to be instructed by him.

"It *is* romantic because it would be so unexpected," Constance explained, a fanciful expression on her heart-shaped face. "A young lady—perhaps an indentured servant—goes to buy the family bread. While there, she chances to meet a sea captain, on leave for a few days only. They look into each other's eyes, and the captain falls instantly in love with her! He pays off her indenture, and they marry at once."

Helen managed to turn a disbelieving laugh into a cough. "And then he goes off for months at a time, forgets to send her any money, and she's worse off than she was before, for now she has a landlord dunning her and nothing to eat."

Constance stared at Helen in astonishment, seemingly at a loss for words.

"It doesn't fit with my experience of life," Helen admitted. "Nothing ever works out so neatly."

"It did for your sister," Constance argued.

Helen didn't bother to hide her laugh. "David was odious to Cassandra and me when we first met. He didn't want anything to do with us. It was only after he saw how perfect she is that he melted."

"That was still very unlikely then, wasn't it? And that proves that two people could fall in love in front of a bread stall."

"Perhaps." Helen adjusted her gray wool cloak and continued on, though she was not precisely sure what to do.

"It would be just the thing for a romance!"

Helen thought she recognized the man standing at the end of the row.

"Oh, no!" she muttered.

"I say it would," Constance replied, wounded.

"No, not your story. Quick, walk this way."

Captain Carter's broad shoulders encased in his customary stark black coat stood out even in the crowded market. For the moment he was busy writing in a little notebook. They might be able to slip by him without notice.

Helen steered Constance around him, striding purposefully, as if she had a very important destination ahead.

"Good morning," a deep voice said.

Helen sighed and turned around. "Captain Carter." She

supposed her fetching cap ribbons had drawn his attention. She shouldn't have fed her vanity by keeping her hood down.

"Oh!" Constance looked up at him like he was a character who had stepped right off the page of a romance.

Even Helen would admit he was very handsome. He had a form like a classical statue, and his full head of hair made the absence of a wig seem no matter. It was a shame that his outward appearance did not match the inner person.

Constance elbowed Helen hard in the stomach and cast her eyes repeatedly towards Captain Carter.

Helen begrudgingly obliged her cousin. "This is Captain Carter. Captain Carter, this is Miss Constance Hayes."

Constance beamed at him and curtsied deeply, while Helen's curtsy could have been mistaken for a small spasm in her leg.

A man as rude in spirit as Captain Carter had no business bowing as elegantly as he did. "Pleased to make your acquaintance. Do I guess correctly—you are doing the work of the Young Ladies of Philadelphia?"

Helen prayed silently for patience. "Philadelphia Young Ladies Charitable Society," she managed to say.

"Yes, we have been walking to and fro quite as much as the adversary himself trying to find a place to sell our gooseberry tarts," Constance quipped. Helen hadn't had occasion to notice such a broad smile grace the captain's face during the entire three years of their acquaintance.

Constance seemed much more attuned to the conversation than she had been all day. Helen wondered if her cousin was fixing Captain Carter in her mind as the hero of the romance she was dreaming about. This was not to be borne.

"We really must continue on. Good day." Helen started to proceed onward, but Constance did not follow.

"The owners who sell in this part of the market hold their spaces very dear. How much have you to spend?" Captain Carter sounded as if he were truly concerned, but Helen guessed he was searching for another opportunity to offer the benefit of his advice.

"Less than a pound," Constance confided.

Helen sniffed. Constance seemed perfectly willing to give away all of the business of the society to a perfect stranger. Would that he would mind his own business and that her cousin would mind her tongue!

"The only place that would give you space at that rate would be in the fish market, but of course you wouldn't want that."

"That's exactly where we're headed, incidentally," Helen lied.

Nathaniel laughed outright as if she'd made an excellent joke. "Nobody is going to buy slices of gooseberry pie surrounded by the stench of fish, even if you could convince the Charitable Ladies to stomach it long enough to hawk their wares."

"Everyone likes tarts," Helen retorted. She didn't appreciate being made sport of. "Once our reputation for selling the best-tasting pastries in Philadelphia grows, we'll have customers lined up for miles, fish or no fish!"

He stared at her incredulously. "Ah, well, you are certainly the expert. A lowly businessman such as I could not dream to teach you anything about business you do not already know." Nathaniel swept another bow and started off in the other direction, shoulders stiff.

Constance stared after him. "I think you've offended him."

"Come. It's rude to stare at a gentleman." Helen glanced back at Captain Carter. "Well, a man, anyway. I'm not certain you could call Captain Carter a gentleman," she muttered to herself. What did he have to be offended about?

The cousins hurried two blocks to the fish market. The odor was overpowering long before they could see the stalls.

Constance pulled her kerchief over her nose. "Are you certain about this?"

Helen was determined not to gag. "Of course. I barely notice the smell."

Blood soaked the tables while flies buzzed around entrails in swarms, so Helen nearly despaired of finding a suitable spot as they walked down the long rows.

She was about to give up when she spotted a small, empty hut at the end of a row. "Excuse me?" she called into the next stall over.

"Aye?"

"Do you know who owns this stall?" Helen pointed to the empty hut.

"Aye."

A long silence ensued. "Might you tell me who?"

The sound of retching made her turn around. Constance was losing her last meal onto the pavement. Helen thought she was in danger of doing so herself, so overpowering was the fishy odor.

"'Tis mine."

"Would you rent it to me?" Helen managed to croak.

The man stared at her as if he did not understand what she was saying. Helen was horrified to realize he had fish bones and gore in his long beard.

She took one step backwards. This had been a terrible idea.

"Two shillings. Roof leaks when it rains."

"Oh, that is an excellent price! I mean, it seems very fair." Helen had a feeling she should just leave as she'd intended, but this price was too good to pass up. They would still have funds left over for ingredients!

"We'll start on Monday. I'll bring the money with me. Good day!" She had to get Constance out of here—she could not seem to cease vomiting.

Helen managed to get Constance home. To her relief, the Hayes family did not seem terribly surprised to see her cousin's pale face, saying she'd always possessed a weak stomach. Perhaps the other girls would manage to overcome the fish scent after getting used to it. After apologizing profusely, Helen retreated to her own home.

The day had not ended auspiciously, but setbacks were to be expected. As long as she persisted, all would be well—and if she could keep certain interfering persons from preventing her.

Nathaniel tried to shake off his irritating encounter with Helen. He'd been civil to her and offered sound advice, yet she'd responded by scorning him—again. He couldn't remember anyone, not even his fiercest competitors, treating him such. Even her dreamy cousin had attended more closely to his words than Helen had.

Her behavior defied logical thought. He must cast her from his mind.

The sign over the door of the Devil's Punchbowl was so dirty he walked past the tavern a few times before finally recognizing it as his destination. The entrance required a step down into an establishment reminiscent of a dungeon.

With no windows, and smoke rolling out of the fireplace, it was nearly impossible to make out who anyone was. He hoped the infernal character of the place was not an ill omen.

Previously he'd been able to hire any number of day laborers to bring in his cargo, all legal and aboveboard. Now that the governor was putting his foot down, he had to find men who knew how to evade the constabulary.

"Carter?" a voice rasped.

"Aye?"

"Matlack." The man didn't offer his hand before planting himself in the chair opposite Nathaniel. He was grizzled from too many days in the sun, with dirty white hair and several long scars across his face.

"I need delivery of forty chests from my ship in Chester to a warehouse in the city," Carter ventured. Best to get to the point and leave this awful place as quickly as possible.

"The kind of delivery that takes place at night when no one else is around, I presume?"

"Aye," Nathaniel confirmed.

Matlack leaned forward. "And you're prepared to pay?"

"Upon delivery." Nathaniel had been in business long enough to know not to trust the man sitting before him with as much as a penny before the goods were safely in his warehouse.

Matlack pulled out a large knife and started cleaning under his nails. "My men won't be too keen on putting their faith in you."

Nathaniel inclined his head. "Nevertheless, I won't pay until the tea is delivered."

"My men will want to know if you'll talk all over town and bring the governor on our heads."

Nathaniel snorted. "Hardly; I've no desire to be caught smuggling."

"You'll ride along with us," Matlack insisted.

"Very well." That suited Nathaniel fine: he'd be able to see that his tea didn't disappear.

"And you'll have one of your men at the docks to signal all clear," Matlack added. "Two lanterns if it's safe and one if it's not. If it's not safe, we dump the cargo and speed back to Chester before the constable can round us up."

Nathaniel paused. He didn't really have many employees that worked for him consistently besides his captains, who hired their own crews. Captain Jones was in town, but Nathaniel would have to pay him very well to keep quiet about this.

"Problem?" Matlack leered at him, and Nathaniel suppressed a shiver.

"No problem." He would find someone.

Matlack spat into his hand and extended it to Nathaniel, who omitted his own secretion but shook nonetheless.

He wandered out into the street and pondered what to do about the man at the dock.

Perhaps David was right that he should just forget about the tea. He could simply dump it and send the *Good King George* to Europe for a legal product. Every day the ship sat in the harbor at Chester he was losing money.

The potential profit was enormous if he could avoid getting caught. The newly taxed legal tea imports hadn't even arrived yet, so shopkeepers were already running low on tea and were willing to pay more than usual. He stood to make a nice profit for himself and his investors. If he could only pull this off one time, he wouldn't have to attempt it again.

He was certain he could do this. He'd managed to work his way up from cabin boy to captain to owner by the age of twenty-nine. After securing his first position, his uncle had not interceded in his life again, and Nathaniel had learned to rely on himself, to stay alert to the way others achieved success and copy them.

He'd thought to help Helen by offering her advice that

would've helped when he was starting out. He wouldn't make that mistake again. Still, he couldn't help but admire her spirit. In a way, she almost reminded him of himself—at least in her determination to succeed, though she was going about it all the wrong way.

Ridiculous. They were absolutely nothing alike. He pushed her firmly out of his mind and started back to his office, pondering who he could ask to help him at the docks.

Chapter 4

Helen invaded the apartment kitchen the moment Peggy left to take her half day, seizing the perfect chance to attempt to decipher Mama's receipt book and produce a fine tart.

"What's a 'goodly' amount of goose fat?" she wondered aloud. She picked through the cabinet where Peggy kept all the ingredients. This looked like the goose fat she remembered, but she couldn't be sure. She dipped one finger in. It smelled like animal. She took a long wooden spoon and scooped a large amount into her mixing bowl.

"Add a good measure of flour," she continued. She shoveled in several heaping spoonfuls of flour and tried to mix the ingredients together with the wooden spoon. The mixture was thick and difficult to stir. She attempted to roll it into a circle, but it was too sticky to hold, so instead she pressed the concoction into a shallow pan.

After digging a few minutes in the pantry Helen managed to locate gooseberry jam and spooned all of it over the crust. She picked up the pan and carried it over to the beehive oven in the corner only to realize it was cold. It took several attempts to get the fire to stay lit, but as soon as a blaze was going, she placed the tart inside and closed the wooden door.

Sighing, she turned to see the table covered in flour and sticky dough. Peggy would be furious to come home to this mess. Helen scraped and wiped the table over and over until it was finally clean, then went to pump more water so Peggy would not notice the bucket had been depleted.

Hoping it was ready, Helen opened the door to the oven and checked on the tart. It resembled a three-day-old stew—globs of gooseberry jam swam in puddles of greasy liquid, and pieces of the crust had bubbled like dumplings.

Helen didn't think it should look like that, but perhaps it hadn't cooked fully. She would go and prepare a gown for Euphemia's concert that evening while she waited for the tart to finish.

She had difficulty choosing between a green velvet robe and the pink silk she'd worn to David's birthday dinner. She was about to ask Cassandra's opinion when the sound of raised voices startled her back into the kitchen.

"What in the name of the Almighty has happened?" Peggy screamed.

"Oh, the tart!" Helen wailed, running forward to throw open the oven door. Black smoke rolled off the surface of the tart in waves. Westing jumped forward and began fanning furiously at the smoke with a cloth.

"Get out of me way!" Peggy yelled, pushing Helen aside and grabbing at the tart with her bare hands. Helen gaped at the cook, who seemed to have hands made of iron.

"What's going on here?" David appeared in the door, waving smoke and coughing.

"My tart—" Helen began.

David didn't let her finish. "We must open all the windows." He and Westing disappeared into the corridor and Helen ran to throw the door to the apartment open. Below, standing at the entrance of his law office, stood Uncle Josiah.

"Is anything the matter?" he inquired.

"Just a burnt tart," Helen explained, coughing in her sleeve. "We have everything under control."

Another gentleman stepped out from behind Uncle Josiah. Governor Morley! Helen was mortified.

"My apologies," she muttered, stepping back into the apartment and hoping he did not recognize her.

The sound of a low moan had her running down the corridor. She burst into Cassandra's room without waiting to knock. Her sister was kneeling over a chamber pot, moaning and retching.

"You've made her very ill," David snapped. He had a hand on Cassandra's back.

"I'm sorry—may I—" Helen took two steps into the room.

David scowled at her. "Just leave us alone!"

Helen spun and ran from the room to her own. Her bedroom was very small compared to the room she had occupied on her father's estate in England, though she knew it had once been shared by several of the Hayes girls when the family lived above Uncle Josiah's law office. She threw herself on her bed, stared at the ceiling, and tried to determine what she should do next. Should she admit defeat?

Captain Carter hadn't thought she could do it.

Helen sat up. Captain Carter was wrong. He might know something about teas and silks, but he was not an expert in tarts.

Euphemia was also supposed to practice baking. Perhaps she had succeeded. Helen would go to her concert and sample a lovely tart, and all would be well.

Nathaniel went back and forth all afternoon and into the early evening, talking himself in and out of attending a concert held at the home of one of his biggest investors. He decided in the end he couldn't afford to anger the man—particularly when he might not be able to return his investment if this tea business blew up.

He honored his host by changing into the coat he saved for important occasions—black, like his everyday coat, but with embossed silver buttons. Helen would probably find fault with his clothing, if she was even attending the concert, but perhaps he could avoid her.

A servant admitted him into the home and led him to the library, where Humphrey Goodwin and the other male guests were drinking spirits before the musical portion of the evening.

"Ah, Carter." Goodwin thumped Nathaniel's back. "I despaired of seeing you tonight, but you're much too shrewd a businessman to risk offending me! Not that I blame you for wanting to stay away. From what I've heard of her lessons, Euphemia has improved since last year's concert, but sitting through all that nonsense is always a dead bore."

Nathaniel wasn't sure how to respond, as affirming his host's words seemed ungentlemanly.

"Nathaniel." David joined their party by the door of the library.

"How are the plans proceeding?" Goodwin asked in what he thought was a low voice.

"Fine," Nathaniel muttered, scratching his neck. He'd been forced to take Humphrey into his confidence against his will when the man had stormed his office demanding what he intended to do about the governor's order.

"Did you manage to find a route?" David whispered.

"Yes, and a team of men who are used to working silently in the dark."

David's eyebrows raised. "Do I want to know?"

"I tried very hard not to inquire too closely about their past activities," Nathaniel said wryly. He was fairly confident they were pirates.

"Oh-ho, that will show old Morley!" Goodwin exclaimed.

David stiffened and tipped his head. "Remember, the man's son is sitting just there."

Nathaniel glanced across the room. Winthrop Morley stared right at them.

"Let him hear," Goodwin chortled. "Morley's not a bad fellow, but he's overstepped this time. The colonies need more leeway than Parliament allows for. If Morley can't keep the peace, he'll be replaced."

David rocked on his heels. "My wife's aunt and uncle are closely connected to the governor, and I've dined with him more than once. He's a very pleasant man to converse with. He's seen an opportunity to line his own pocket and means to take it. It really is no different than what we are doing."

"Morley won't suffer if this business doesn't come off in his favor, but I will," Nathaniel argued. "He can't expect to suddenly open his eyes to the smuggling that has gone on for years under his nose and have everyone submit meekly to new restrictions."

"I just can't like this business of smuggling. I fear it will end in disaster."

"Smuggling is so common in the colonies that it's practically patriotic," Nathaniel retorted.

David shrugged. "It's gotten too dangerous. I believe there's another way."

Goodwin broke in. "Say you don't mean relying on the Sons of Liberty! They plan to make a demonstration, but it will come to naught just as it always has. Besides, I don't mind depriving the king of a few pounds, but I draw the line at rebellion. These colonies are English land for English people and English rule." He stuck his finger in the air at each utterance of his mother country's name.

Nathaniel couldn't risk offending the man by saying what he thought of King George. While he had no trust in the Sons of Liberty, he also felt no allegiance to a king he'd never seen.

"I daresay you look terribly suspicious there," a voice drawled.

Nathaniel stiffened. Winthrop Morley dressed in a ridiculous manner that Nathaniel could not imagine being in fashion anywhere, and certainly not in Philadelphia. He wore wigs that had more rolls and curls than the king himself if the cartoon images printed in the newspaper were anything to go by.

"We are merely talking of the weather," David lied.

Winthrop smirked. "Of course; there's much to say. How cool it has been, and how characteristic of October." He turned to Nathaniel. "How nice to see you again," he said, making it clear it was anything but nice. "I thought to drop you a little hint. My father wants to discourage any disloyalty to the crown. He'd hoped that merely confiscating the ill-gotten goods of would-be smugglers would suffice, but he's heard rumors that not everyone finds that sufficient motivation. Tomorrow he'll make an announcement." He paused for dramatic effect. "Anyone caught smuggling will have *all* his assets seized on behalf of the crown."

Nathaniel and David exchanged a glance. Previously, the cost of smuggling was a fine and the loss of that ship's cargo. Losing everything was a significantly harsher penalty.

Goodwin snorted. "Your father should take care not to strike a match that will send the whole tinderbox up in flame."

"My father is loyal to the king, and the king will reward that loyalty." Winthrop took a sip of his drink.

A servant appeared at Goodwin's side.

"Miss Euphemia says she means to come down soon, and she'd like all the gentlemen to be seated."

"I am loyal to my king, gentlemen," Goodwin said, "But I obey my daughter. Follow me!"

Helen arrived early to Euphemia's concert and was immediately led up to her friend's bedroom.

"Right through here. Miss Euphemia says you're to come in."

"Oh, Helen!" Euphemia called. She ran over to hug Helen. "I can't wait to show you what I made! Isn't it wonderful?" She gestured towards the middle of her dressing table, where her tart sat amidst ribbons and pins.

Helen stared at Euphemia's tart in dismay. It looked like a dry biscuit spread thinly with jam.

"Do you wish to try some?" Euphemia offered.

"Not right now," Helen managed to say.

"Yes, I should probably finish getting dressed. I had no notion I could make something like this with my own hands! I see you are quite touched as well."

Euphemia mistook Helen's tears as admiration. "Take this away," she motioned to a maid, holding her arms wide so her lady's maid could finish robing her. She'd already donned an impressive set of panniers that would have been suitable for an audience with the queen.

Distraught as she was, Helen could not help but admire the gold petticoat as her maid lowered it over Euphemia's head, taking care not to disrupt her elaborate hairstyle.

What was Helen to do? Euphemia's tart was no more edible than hers. She was certain Verity Hayes could produce edible specimens, but could she be relied upon to make all the tarts for the sale? How was Helen to go before the society and explain that she'd failed?

"How many tarts do you suppose I'll need to make each day?" Euphemia asked, patiently waiting for her robe to be pinned in place. It was also gold, but embroidered all over with large golden harps.

"I—" Helen began, distracted by the clothing. "What a remarkable gown."

"I had it made especially for this evening! Do you like it?"

"Very singular. I can't recall how many tarts we'll need; I have it recorded somewhere. . . ." Her mind was too disordered to give Euphemia an exact number. Should they call the whole thing off?

"I had no idea how much I would love being in the kitchen. I'm prepared to drop everything to make as many tarts as you need. Music lessons, dancing lessons, carriage rides, morning visits—I'm willing to sacrifice it all for our noble cause!"

"Admirable," Helen muttered. She managed to excuse herself to go find a seat.

Euphemia beamed. "Wonderful! I'll be down soon."

Helen walked slowly down the Goodwins' wide wooden staircase, heart sinking further with every step. She was starting to wonder if there was any way to recover the operation.

In the drawing room, most of the guests were already assembled waiting for Euphemia to arrive. Elegant gilt chairs faced a large harpsichord at the front of the room.

David had just returned from wherever the men were congregating. He sat down on the other side of Cassandra without greeting Helen.

Cassandra had difficulty speaking without coughing. "How was the tart?" she croaked, clutching her rounded stomach gently.

Helen was unsure how to answer. "She made a sincere effort."

David harrumphed. "Bad as yours, then?"

"All will be well," Helen insisted, though she scarcely believed this.

"It's hardly to be believed that some people have the sheer effrontery—" David began.

"Helen, is your fichu coming loose? Perhaps we should go tuck it in," Cassandra interrupted.

"No need to get up; I'll go by myself," Helen nearly ran from the room, barely managing to sneak behind Captain Carter, who was talking to her uncle. He was the last person she wanted to see at this time. He'd probably tell her exactly how she'd done everything wrong, which she already knew well enough.

Why had she agreed to serve as president? Was she really so delusional to have believed she could organize this? She would fail, and that poor indentured girl would be doomed to total ruin. All because Helen was just as inept as Captain Carter thought she was.

She felt the tears starting and ducked into the first unoccupied room she found in order to cry.

Chapter 5

Nathaniel had accomplished what he came to do—speak to his host—and now he wondered if he needed to wait for an intermission to slip out or if he could manage it sooner.

He bowed to Josiah Hayes as the man entered the drawing room behind him. He didn't know the man very well, but they had met a few times since David's wedding a few years ago.

Hayes bowed in return. "Mr. Carter. It's good to see you. I won't ask you how business is going, for I know this is a troublesome time for men in your line."

Nathaniel could not resist replying, "As it's a lucrative time for men in your line."

Hayes chuckled. "Young man, it's always a lucrative time for those of us in the law. Human nature dictates that men are forever cheating and fighting each other." He patted Nathaniel on the shoulder and sought his seat next to his wife and daughters. One of the Hayes daughters—Nathaniel didn't know them well enough to know which—appeared to be enacting a stage show maneuvering to sit next to Winthrop Morley.

Euphemia swept into the room once everyone was seated. A hush fell over the assembled guests as she sat down at the harpsichord. She bowed her head as if in prayer and then threw her hands on the keys.

She had admittedly improved since last year, but Nathaniel had to agree with Humphrey that this kind of music was not to his taste.

A minute later David made his way down the aisle supporting his wife. Nathaniel decided to see if he could be of assistance—and possibly leave.

"Everything all right?" he asked, once a servant closed the door off behind him.

"Cassandra's not feeling very well, so we are leaving. May I trouble you to see Helen home? She's disappeared somewhere in this house."

"I can manage—" Cassandra said weakly, before breaking down into a coughing fit.

"Your sister nearly murdered you! I think she's the one who must manage."

Attempted murder? Nathaniel hoped that was an exaggeration. He didn't want to spend any more time than he had to in Helen's company but felt he couldn't refuse. "Very well," he agreed reluctantly.

David flashed a small smile. "I won't forget it." He ushered his wife outside.

Nathaniel had seen Helen dash from the room while he spoke to Hayes. If he could find her, perhaps she would also want to leave early when she heard about her sister and he could escape from the party by escorting her home.

He made his way down the corridor of the main floor. He knew from previous experience that the dining room was behind a pair of ornate double doors, but it seemed unlikely Helen was there.

Perhaps she was in the library? He turned the knob slowly and pushed the door open. Helen sat, head in hands, on the couch Winthrop had lounged in earlier.

For a moment he considered turning to leave. She would probably find this just as awkward as he did. Then he recalled his promise to see her safe and rallied his courage.

"Are you—" he began.

Helen sat up quickly. "Oh! It's you. Probably here to laugh at my downfall." Her face was swollen.

Nathaniel couldn't decipher her meaning. "Laugh at your downfall?" he repeated.

Helen drew a shaky breath. "There's no chance the society will succeed with me as president." She hid her face in her hands again, shoulders shaking.

Nathaniel had no experience with this many tears—not even the cabin boys who had worked on his ships cried like this. Probably best to take a firm hand.

"Nonsense," he tried. "It can't be as bad as that."

"Oh, it can't, can it? Today I discovered I'm a terrible cook when I nearly burned down our apartment and killed my only sister. Then I pinned my hopes on Euphemia's tart, but hers was just as bad!"

"So—you have a product deficiency?" he translated.

Helen nodded, trying to wipe her eyes on the edge of her sleeve.

Nathaniel offered her a handkerchief which she accepted without comment. At least she didn't refuse it. "Why don't you ask your cooks to produce the tarts?"

Helen dabbed her eyes. "We want to do all the work ourselves to show we are able to manage the whole business on our own."

"I don't produce the goods I sell," Nathaniel pointed out. "I don't believe anyone has questioned me."

"You're a man," Helen retorted. "You could have no employment at all and yet men would not question your worth."

Nathaniel shook his head, thinking of Winthrop, but he did not want to bring him into the conversation.

"I doubt any of your customers are like to inquire much into the origins of the tart so long as the taste is good," he pressed.

"Perhaps. But that leaves the matter of the stall. Constance was made so ill by the smell she didn't recover for days."

Nathaniel couldn't hide a grin. "I did warn you."

Helen looked up at him, eyes flashing. "Why mention the fish market at all if you did not intend to bait me to go there?"

Nathaniel was puzzled. "You speak as if we are in competition."

Helen stared at him but said nothing.

He withdrew his notebook and a pencil stub from an interior pocket of his coat. "How much money does the society have?"

"Only a shilling."

"And the rent at one of the better stalls is how much?"

"Two pounds."

"How long do you intend to rent it?"

"I hadn't thought . . . perhaps just the month?"

Nathaniel refrained from commenting on her lack of planning and wrote down the numbers. "And your ingredients—how much does it cost you to make one tart?"

Helen stared at him blankly. "I don't know."

"You must find out, and that will determine how much you must charge for each slice. You must charge enough that you can make a profit, but not so much that no one will buy. I'll be your investor and lend you three pounds, and the society will pay me back a percentage each week until you have paid off the loan."

"It will take us longer to earn the money if we have to pay a portion to you and a portion to the baker," Helen protested.

Nathaniel waved this away. "Yes, but you will sell more tarts if you're in a better location. Now, at first, you'll make too many tarts, or too few, so you must keep a record of your sales so you may learn to anticipate your market."

Helen didn't answer right away. "I'd not planned to seek any assistance."

"It's sound business practice to make use of every opportunity." He hadn't intended to give her any more unsolicited advice, but she seemed amenable at the moment.

The door to the library burst open, and Euphemia swept into the room. "Oh, Helen! I thought you'd left. Why—oh! I'm sorry if I interrupted something. I'd no idea of disturbing a *tête-à-tête*! But—it can't be proper for you to remain alone here for too much longer! Why, no one has come to light the lamps, and the fire is getting low. How can you stand to sit in the dark?"

Nathaniel jumped up. "I'm sorry. I forgot to mention to you that your sister had to leave early and I am to see you home."

"Oh dear. I must go to her."

"I can send a boy around to the stables for our coach," Euphemia offered.

Helen considered this. "No, walking will be faster. Unless you mind walking?"

"I'm very fond of walking." He watched in surprise as Helen embraced Euphemia. If a man let him down in business, he would certainly not expect to receive a hug for it.

Helen retrieved her cloak. "Ready?"

They emerged onto the street, and Nathaniel wondered if he should offer her his arm. Would she accept it? He didn't want to appear uncouth by not offering. Nor did he want to be rejected. Was it forward? He had so little experience of women. He deliberated too long—it would have been awkward to offer now. What could he say to relieve the silence?

Finally Helen spoke. "Thank you for seeing me home—and for the advice. I daresay you think I'm hopeless at business."

"I made a great deal of mistakes when I began. I knew a lot about ships and sailing but nothing about selling. I lost money on the first cargo I ever brought in as owner."

"Oh. How did you learn?"

"By observation and asking questions, and from learning from my mistakes and not repeating them." He hoped that would be a lesson to her. All of a sudden he realized Helen was actually attending to him, not bristling as she always had before.

"Shall I see you up?" he asked as they reached her home. He wouldn't mind discussing her plans further.

"Oh no, I mustn't detain you further. Thank you. Good night." She turned quickly to open the door of the law office.

"Wait—I'll call on you. To discuss the business, I mean."

"Oh, yes," she agreed. "Good night!"

Nathaniel walked slowly home. What made him offer to invest in the society business? As a rule, he thought indenture contracts were between servant and master. He'd seen her weeping and panicked and had not known what he was supposed to do.

He should've just told her about Cassandra's illness and escorted her home. Helen's problems were no concern of his, and he had enough of his own to contend with. According to Winthrop, Governor Morley wouldn't stop at taking the tea: he'd seize everything Nathaniel owned if he caught him. He would give Helen the money and stay out of the business. No more help. No more distractions.

Chapter 6

Helen didn't want to ask anyone for help, but she couldn't carry eight gooseberry tarts all the way to the market without damaging them, so she had to resort to asking David for the use of his coach.

"Am I to consider this an investment to be repaid?" he asked as he handed the tarts up to her.

"Consider it a charitable contribution." Being teased didn't make it any easier to accept assistance. He'd offered to send Westing with her, but she assured David she could do this on her own. She hadn't even had to ask Peggy for help with baking. She'd only had to pretend to warm herself by the kitchen fire and observe Peggy's technique while she prepared a dried cherry pie. After that, baking tarts became much easier.

David's coach had to let her out on the street a hundred yards from the market. The stall was a fair distance away, and Helen was forced to leave six of her tarts in the coach while she carried the first two.

"I must get a large basket," she muttered to herself. Jane

and Patience had already arrived. They had only made four tarts apiece, according to Helen's instructions—she'd not wanted to overburden them. They helped Helen retrieve the six remaining tarts and sent the coach on its way. Helen hurried, worried customers would be lined up and waiting for them, but the stall was empty when they arrived.

"Perhaps all our customers are enjoying a relaxed morning," Helen suggested. "Well, let's see what everyone made!" She pulled the towel off one of the tarts. "Oh—are those gooseberries?"

"No, we had no more jam, so I had to use dried blueberries," Jane explained.

Helen had given very precise instructions because she wanted everything to be perfect. Jane should have made more of an effort to ensure she had the right ingredients.

"Did you make these yourself?" she asked Patience, continuing her examination.

"Oh, no. Verity did. She's a wonder in the kitchen!"

"It must be a comfort to come from such a talented family. Now," Helen said, hoping she sounded both friendly and commanding, "I hope you both read my letter carefully. We must make an effort to be precise."

Just then, a customer walked up to their stall. Helen nearly tripped over their small table in her attempts to approach the woman. "Good day! Would you like to buy a slice of tart?"

The woman, marked as a servant by her cropped wool bedgown, stared at Helen for a moment and then motioned at the baker. "I'm here for the bread."

"Of course," Helen mumbled, stepping back. "Jane, you prepare the plates," she whispered. "Patience, start slicing one of the tarts."

Patience dutifully pulled one of the pastries closer and lifted a knife.

"No—not that one," Helen hissed. "We'll save the blueberry for when we run out of gooseberry."

Jane pulled a stack of porcelain plates from a basket beneath their feet. "Oh, I thought I said to bring tin plates so we didn't run the risk of breaking any crockery."

"My mother said she can spare these, as my younger sisters have already broken several in the set," Patience explained. Helen drew in another sharp breath. Was it so difficult to follow simple instructions?

Another customer approached the stall but didn't make eye contact with them. Helen peered up and down the market row. There were many people shopping, but no one showed any interest in tarts. What if they sold nothing?

At that moment, Anne Hayes arrived with her other four daughters.

Aunt Anne admired the tarts and took Helen's hands. "Oh, how lovely! You've arranged everything beautifully. Now, we would like to purchase five slices."

Helen blinked. She'd only asked Jane and Patience to bring two plates a piece. She'd been through all the dishes at the apartment, but David didn't have a single tin plate in his home.

Temperance pulled the cloth off one of Jane's tarts. "Oh, is that blueberry? I want that!"

Helen tried not to glare at Temperance. It was truly surprising that a person who aspired to be at the top of society would select a less fashionable dessert.

Jane gave out four plates. Aunt Anne's eyes roved over the table, and then she looked back at her plate.

"We don't have any utensils," Helen explained. "You have to eat with your hands." As she spoke, her stomach knotted. In her mind the customers had been perfectly able to pick up the tart and eat it neatly, but it shortly became evident this was impossible as she watched the slices fall apart the moment the ladies tried to lift them.

"Where's my piece?" Verity asked. "I should get at least one slice of my own tart!"

"Just as soon as we have a free plate." Temperance and Aunt Anne exchanged a look and started to eat faster.

"You can have mine," Constance said, passing her plate to Verity. "The memory of my last trip to this market makes me unable to muster an appetite."

Mercy, the youngest Hayes daughter, finished first and returned her plate. "That was very good."

"Yes," agreed Aunt Anne. "Excellent tart!"

"So filling," Temperance said, leaving a half-eaten slice.

They stood in awkward silence watching Verity finish Constance's slice. When she was finished, she gave the plate back and examined her sticky fingers.

Another man came up behind the family. "Excuse me," he said. "I need to get by."

Aunt Anne quickly took Mercy by the hand and motioned her daughters onward. "Well, we wish you the best of luck! Goodbye, dears."

Patience stared at the dirty plates. "How are we to wash them?"

Helen hadn't thought of that. "Excuse me?" she asked the baker. "Do you have any water?"

"Water pump is two rows that direction. If you have a bucket." He was so taciturn that Helen was afraid to ask to borrow any kind of vessel.

"We'll just wipe them clean," she whispered, reaching for a plate. She started wiping them with one of the towels they were using to cover the tarts. Not knowing what else to do, she threw Temperance's half-eaten piece behind the little table they were using.

The next customers were friends of Jane's. Helen supposed they must be fellow Quakers, for they dressed very plain. They did justice to the dessert, however, and even complimented Helen's gooseberry tart, which disposed her to think very favorably of them.

Midday saw the ladies hungry and a little cold from being outside so long. The baker had a little stove where he warmed himself, but the heat didn't extend to where they stood, and he didn't offer to let them stand closer.

"Perhaps we might take it in turns to walk up and down to warm up a bit?" Jane suggested.

Helen agreed; thus when they had their largest crowd yet, there were only two of them to try to take the money, serve the slices of tart, and surreptitiously wipe the plates clean.

"Workers in search of dinner," Patience noted. "Perhaps they will return and bring others tomorrow."

Helen's fingers drummed on the table. "We'll need more plates."

Several of Uncle Josiah's clerks came next and made eyes at Patience. "Are you here to make a purchase?" Helen finally asked, and that goaded them into each buying a slice. One of the clerks hustled the rest away.

At first it seemed they would shortly sell out of tarts, but by late afternoon business had slowed down again, and there were still four gooseberry tarts left. The less fashionable had consumed the blueberry.

"I'm sorry, but I have to go to a meeting." Jane apologized. "I can't stay any longer."

"It's no matter. Thank you for your assistance." Helen turned to Patience. "It's just you and I!"

Patience bit her lip. "I've a lute lesson."

"I'm certain I can manage," Helen lied. She wasn't certain of any such thing.

The baker just packed up without saying anything at all.

She wanted to sell all the remaining tarts before leaving. Perhaps she should start calling out like they did in the meat section of the market. She felt something squish under her foot and realized she was stepping in the discarded pile of half-eaten tart.

She should've written down the times they sold the most slices. Captain Carter had told her to keep records and even left her with a new notebook when he brought her the money for the loan.

"Do I need to include this in the loan repayment?" she'd asked, but he said it was a gift.

He was a puzzle to her. She'd thought men were prone to run the other way when confronted by crying women. Instead, he'd spoken to her gently and helped her find a better plan. It was not at all in keeping with what she knew of him.

"Are there any pies for sale?" Helen looked up to see Nathaniel Carter standing in front of her.

"We have tarts," she corrected, determined to be polite despite his error, as he was a potential customer. "Gooseberry tarts. Would you like a slice?"

Nathaniel considered the tart in front of him. "I'm not much for sweet foods."

That was *her* tart he found unappealing. "I'm sorry this isn't to your liking. Perhaps you can be prevailed upon to make a donation despite your disgust."

Nathaniel frowned and reached into his coat pocket. "How much?"

"Two pence."

He laid them on the table, then abruptly turned and walked away.

Helen threw both hands in the air. To think she'd thought he was softening!

It was not yet dark when most of the stalls had closed and Helen realized it was not worth freezing herself when she was unlikely to have any more customers. She stacked all the tarts and tins together and started walking to the edge of the market.

Two men stood conversing at the end of the row—Governor Morley and his son. Helen just wanted to seek a warm seat by the fire and tried to curtsy without stopping. She soon heard footsteps and turned to see Winthrop Morley behind her.

Winthrop removed his tricornered hat and bowed elaborately, head nearly touching the ground. "You are Josiah Hayes's niece, I believe?"

"Y-yes," Helen said, shivering violently, as it was impossible to hold her cloak closed and carry so many tart tins at the same time.

"I thought I recognized you. I'd no idea Lord David's situation had grown so dire!" He motioned to the tarts.

"Oh—no—this is for charity. The Philadelphia Young Ladies Charitable Society."

Winthrop's eyes narrowed. "You're selling pies to raise funds?"

"Tarts."

Winthrop glanced around. Besides his father, standing a few yards off, they were alone. "Where are you selling them?"

"We've rented a space in a corner of a merchant stall." Why was he so interested? Couldn't he leave her alone so she could get home and warm up?

"I take it you are unaware you must pay a fee to register your business?"

Helen blinked at him. "I was not aware. How much is the fee?"

"One pound." Winthrop drummed his fingers against his

hat. "In addition to a five percent tax on all goods sold. If you have the money now, I'll be happy to take it with me.

"Oh, but that is so much, you can't possibly—this money is for a very good cause!" Helen stammered.

"Your king's service is the noblest cause of all." He held out a hand.

Helen was too cold to think and just wanted to get this over with quickly. She set the tins down on the ground and pulled her money pouch out of her pocket. Winthrop grabbed it from her, counted out two pounds and put the rest of the pence back into her purse.

"Wait just a moment!" Helen began, but Winthrop was already turning away. "That's not five percent!" He'd taken more than half what they earned, and some of that money was what Nathaniel lent her.

"Your king has need of it." He bowed again and returned to his father.

Helen stomped her foot. This was ridiculous! She hurried home as fast as she could, but it was full dark by the time she arrived.

Cassandra greeted her at the door and helped her carry the leftover tarts into the kitchen. "Come and warm yourself in the drawing room," she urged, leading Helen down the hallway. "How was it?"

Cassandra was properly sympathetic while Helen related everything that happened during the day. "Can you believe the conduct of that odious man?"

"It's hard to credit, as his father is so gentlemanly. Still, one hears such things about Winthrop. David says—well, that's not fit for your ears."

Helen snorted. "He's also odious, but I was talking of Captain Carter!"

"Dear, do you not think you are being a trifle unjust to

him? He didn't want any tart, but he made a donation anyway."

"He didn't want *my* tart," Helen argued. "Perhaps it was the color? The tart Patience brought had a deeper color."

"Perhaps he's just shy," Cassandra suggested. "You're very severe on him."

"You used to be also," Helen retorted.

"That was until I knew him better. He has a good heart. First impressions aren't always accurate."

Helen smiled wryly and shook her head. "You want to see the best in everyone since David turned out to be better than you'd imagined. Not everyone is worth getting to know better."

"Perhaps," Cassandra said, not sounding convinced.

"I need to find more plates." Helen tried to stand and thought her legs would buckle beneath her. "Oh, I ache all over!"

"Perhaps you should consider something easier to make and serve than tarts," Cassandra suggested.

Helen waved this away as she left the room. "Jane thought we ought to serve gingerbread, but she has no knowledge of what is fashionable."

Cassandra followed her into the corridor. "Perhaps that's not the most essential thing to consider in this case."

"Perhaps," Helen replied. She needed to smuggle out more plates without anyone noticing.

Cassandra was wrong. Look at how well sales had gone! Eight whole tarts sold to paying customers. She would just have to find a way to avoid Winthrop, and they would have the money in no time.

She'd also have to find a way to avoid Captain Carter. He always managed to leave her confused and unable to focus. She'd planned to repay his investment a little at a time, but perhaps she could pay him sooner and be done with the whole arrangement. After that, the money they raised would all go to paying off the indenture and she would feel comfortable again, without his interference.

Chapter 7

Nathaniel walked around the city, trying to think of who he could ask to stand at the docks the night of the smuggling operation. The sky was gray, indicating the season's first snow would soon fall.

"Good afternoon," someone called, drawing his attention from the weather. Nathaniel looked up to see David approaching and realized he'd ended up right outside the city market.

Nathaniel bowed to David. "What are you doing out here?"

"I'm under assignment from Cassandra to buy up the rest of Helen's tarts for the day. She worries it's far too cold to leave her sister outside until dark."

"Are the tarts selling well, then?" Nathaniel asked, not that he cared other than to ensure his investment was repaid.

"I suppose, though I'll be heartily glad to never see a gooseberry tart again so long as I live. Helen always makes far too many because she's scared of running out." David patted his stomach. "I'll have to take to lacing myself."

Nathaniel chuckled. "She's very determined to succeed."

"Oh, yes. She's awake at all hours making tarts, and she insists upon coming personally to sell on every market day. Cassandra's been beside herself with worry that Helen will make herself sick."

Nathaniel was begrudgingly impressed. "She must feel very strongly about this." He was just as dedicated to his work, and he'd known many men who didn't work half as hard.

"Helen and Cassandra were very nearly sold into indenture by an unscrupulous captain when they arrived in Philadelphia. Helen takes it very personally."

The two men watched Helen and her companion from a distance. They didn't appear to have any customers at the moment. Euphemia Goodwin was talking animatedly while Helen rearranged the tarts laid out before them.

"Perhaps she should continue on in business after they raise the sum they need," Nathaniel suggested.

David snorted. "She'll have to expand her offerings. I believe the city has been emptied of gooseberry jam. Say—what brings you here? Have you been watching over her?"

"What? No. I'm just mulling over a problem with the shipment." Nathaniel lowered his voice. "The group I hired wants me to travel up the river in the boats and they want another of my men to meet them at the docks. They believe this will prevent me from being careless and talking about the plan."

"Who will you choose?"

"I don't know. Most of my 'men' are day-laborers I hire to move my cargo. I can't be certain they wouldn't sell me out to Morley."

"When do you mean to do it?" David asked, still watching Helen.

"Next Friday."

"Ah, the governor's ball."

"Precisely—the one night he should be looking the other direction."

"Have you any friends you could ask?"

Nathaniel shrugged nonchalantly. "Not really, but I'll find someone."

David put a hand on his shoulder. "You can count on me. I'll be there at the docks."

Nathaniel took a step back. "You won't try to talk me out of this?"

"No, you're determined to go forward, and I'm determined to buy a larger house for my growing family with all the money you'll earn for me."

"Thank you. I—" Nathaniel struggled to tell David how much it meant to him to have someone he could depend on.

"What the devil?" David stalked off suddenly towards Helen and Euphemia. Nathaniel followed quickly behind.

Winthrop Morley stood in front of the stall with his hand out while Helen counted out coins. She wasn't happy.

"What's going on here?" David demanded.

Winthrop simpered. "I'm collecting a sales tax."

"There's no sales tax collected at market, only a tariff upon goods entering the city," Nathaniel retorted.

"New ordinance. Applies to new businesses."

"This is hardly a business!" David exclaimed. "This is a group of young ladies selling pies for charity!"

"Tarts," Helen muttered. She stood behind the table with her arms crossed while Euphemia looked on with wide eyes.

"Do you collect this tax of all the stalls?" Nathaniel challenged.

"New businesses, yes. Well, good day! I'll be back tomorrow." Winthrop turned to go but David seized him by the shoulder and spun him around. A few people shopping nearby edged a little closer to the two men. The baker who owned the stall leaned forward, not even pretending he wasn't paying attention to every word.

"This will not stand!" David insisted. "I've not heard of any such ordinance being posted. You outstrip your authority this time."

Winthrop brushed David off. "I think you'll find I do not. Take it up with the magistrate if you must, though I warn you—he's a great friend of my father's. I know I'll certainly speak to him if you lay a hand on me again."

"No need to wait! Name your second," David demanded. Nathaniel caught his breath. Would Winthrop accept that deadly challenge?

Winthrop laughed. "I won't even deign to answer that." He turned and walked away.

"Because he knows I never miss at a hundred paces!" David called out, fuming.

"How dare you?" Helen hissed. "You've drawn a crowd and you'll frighten away all our customers."

David glared at the onlookers, and the handful of people who had stopped turned back to their business. The baker spat and shook his head before returning to stuffing unsold bread into a sack.

"How long has this been going on?" David demanded.

Helen's shoulders drooped. "Every day. I told Cassandra all about it after the first time."

"She mentioned a tax, but I never dreamed he was harassing you like this. That villainous, lecherous—"

"Stop!" Helen hissed. Euphemia leaned in as if she wanted to hear more.

"My father won't allow me to accept even an offer to dance with him. He tried to court me last year, but it was only because I'm a great heiress," Euphemia confided. "What does 'lecherous' mean?"

Helen met Nathaniel's eyes for the first time. "Just that he's like a leach," Helen lied. "Well, we'll sell no more today. Help me gather up these tarts, Euphemia."

"Wait a moment," David said, forcing himself to turn away from Winthrop's retreating form. "I'm sent to purchase a tart for dinner, and I'm certain Nathaniel also wishes to buy."

"You're certain?" Helen's voice was tight. "I'm not. Nathaniel doesn't care for my cooking."

Nathaniel didn't know what to say. He hadn't intended to offend her when he admitted he didn't often eat sweet foods. Without speaking he reached into his coat pocket for his coin purse. He counted out two pence, placed them on the table, and turned to go.

"Wait," David called after him, but Nathaniel kept walking. David jogged to catch up to him. "What was that all about?"

Nathaniel shrugged. "She hates me, though I can't understand why."

"I don't think that's it. You've offended her somehow."

"What?"

David nodded sagely. "I've seen it before in women. What did you say about her pie?"

"Tart," Nathaniel corrected automatically. "I told her the truth; I don't much care for desserts, but I gave her the value of the slice as a donation."

David groaned. "You really have no idea how to talk to ladies, do you? You rejected what she made. She's been wounded!"

"I'm not sure I follow. She's there to make money. I gave her money. What's there to be angry about?"

David laid a hand on Nathaniel's shoulder in a paternal way that was amusing coming from a man near his own age. "Let me explain it like this. Imagine you made her a gift of tea you imported and she said she didn't like the taste."

Was this supposed to be a riddle? "I'd examine the product carefully for defects and seek a refund from my supplier if I found anything amiss."

David groaned. "You're hopeless. She has feelings invested! She's spent time and effort making the product. I don't much care for gooseberries, but I knew enough to compliment her even though I was made to consume three whole tarts by myself!"

"So you're saying I should try the tart and pretend to like it?" Nathaniel clarified.

"Exactly." David beamed at him with a parental sort of pride.

Nathaniel turned to walk back to the stall, but David stopped him with a hand on his arm.

"Not right this moment. It's better to wait until they're calm. This can take days."

None of it made much sense to Nathaniel. "Perhaps you should write a book."

"Not a bad idea. I could share everything I've learned." David stroked his chin.

Nathaniel wished him a good day and returned to his warehouse. He needed to get in touch with Matlack and let him know he'd found a man for the docks.

He was touched by David's offer. He'd always considered David as a business partner, but the man was acting as a true friend to him.

Should he allow a man with a family to put himself at risk? If he was caught helping, David could also lose everything he owned. Helen would certainly blame Nathaniel if that happened.

Despite what David said, Nathaniel was unconvinced Helen would ever warm to him, though she seemed to do so a little that night at the concert. He'd even been moved to make her a present of a notebook to keep accounts in, and she'd seemed happy to accept. Still, nothing else he did pleased her, no matter how hard he tried.

Hot one moment and cold the next. Perhaps David was right that he'd offended her—possibly from the first time they met? Why did she preoccupy his thoughts so? He could at least try to make amends.

Nathaniel rubbed his face and noticed the cuff of one sleeve was starting to unravel. He would have to mend it. His boots needed cleaning as well. He should find a boy to attend to them. All this, and find a place to hide the tea. He groaned and set off for his office.

Chapter 8

Nathaniel threw down his shovel and slid to the floor of his warehouse. He'd spent days searching the city but couldn't find a suitable location to store the tea. Half the places he'd checked were too far from the docks, and the others were too public.

He'd have to use his own warehouse, but he needed a cellar to hide the tea in case the governor came around. Digging was long, hard work, but he couldn't hire someone who might betray him to the governor for a coin. Nathaniel knew better than to ask David to help with manual labor.

He'd ignored his growling stomach, having worked long past the time he would normally pause for dinner. He knew he had to stop when his body started shaking from fatigue. He shrugged back into his coat and tramped through fallen snow to the tavern nearest his warehouse.

The owner of the tavern raised a hand in greeting and brought him a bowl of food. Lamb stew was not Nathaniel's favorite dish, but he forced himself to choke it down.

Nathaniel glanced around the tavern. There was only one

other man sitting by himself. The loner shoveled food into his mouth, never looking up or smiling. Nathaniel hoped he wouldn't end up like that.

David was probably spending the day sitting in front of a large fire, laughing with his pretty wife. Nathaniel could almost imagine it, though he'd not had much experience with family life.

His own father, a wheelwright, had been killed when a cart he was repairing fell on him. He had lived a few weeks after the accident with a putrid wound that never got better. Nathaniel had been only seven. The very next week after his father died, his mother sent him to live with his uncle, a ship's captain, and married a widower with seven children.

She wrote to him a few times admonishing him to be a God-fearing man, which he'd always tried to do. He'd visited her but felt like a stranger in another man's home. He hadn't learned about families from his uncle, who had never married, nor the men he'd sailed with, who didn't much prize monogamy.

Would he be happier with a wife? He never wanted companionship before, but now he thought it would be nice to have someone to return home to at night. Someone he could discuss his work with.

He didn't want someone vapid like Euphemia Goodwin. But then, what woman would have him? He lived in a one-room apartment above a cobbler's shop. He owned a total of two coats, both dull black. He was apparently hopeless at conversing with the entire sex. He could move or buy a new coat, but he doubted he would ever understand women.

Why did Helen's face appear in his mind?

He didn't have time to consider this. He pushed away from the table and headed back to work.

Helen emerged from her room with four pounds wrapped in a letter informing its recipient that her business with him was concluded. She would ask David to accompany her to Nathaniel's warehouse and then slip the note under his door. After that, he would have no reason to come to her stall ever again, and her mind would have no cause to dwell on him continually.

The sound of voices reached her ears before she entered the drawing room. She peered into the room to find Cassandra sitting perched on David's knee while they laughed over something. David had his hand on Cassandra's stomach.

"Do you feel that?" Cassandra asked.

David grinned. "My son!"

"Daughter," Cassandra insisted.

Helen stepped back quickly. She didn't want to intrude.

A quick rummage through the papers on David's desk revealed Nathaniel's address. She'd go by herself and return before anyone missed her. The snow had ceased falling and been cleared off the streets, and it would take less than an hour to make the trip and return home again.

The image of David and Cassandra wouldn't leave her mind. Her heart ached—not with jealousy, but with longing for a companion. She was merely a hanger-on in David's household, sister to his wife and soon-to-be aunt to his child. She didn't think David or Cassandra resented her presence, but likely they would appreciate a chance to live without another adult always lurking about.

She'd had the vague notion that she ought to seek out a husband, only no one had presented himself that she could fathom living with for years on end. In appearance, she could admit that Nathaniel represented everything she found pleasing. Well-built, even-featured—and the way he seemed so still but so aware at the same time. Of course, he obviously didn't think of her in that way at all.

She reached his door and slid the square of paper underneath. The moment she straightened herself up, the door swung open.

Nathaniel stood in the doorway. "Yes?"

"I was just leaving that for you," Helen stammered.

Nathaniel stooped to pick up the paper, and Helen saw an assortment of picks and shovels leaned up against the wall behind him." Are you digging something?" she couldn't resist asking.

Nathaniel glanced at the street behind her. "No, just—"

She knew when she wasn't wanted. "I see. Good day."

"Wait—come in for a moment." Nathaniel stepped back to let her inside.

Helen considered him for a moment, unsure if she wanted to comply. Perhaps it was only Christian of her to allow him the chance to apologize.

Nathaniel looked up and down the street once more as he closed the door behind him. Helen shivered. The dark room was colder than the street, the only light coming from a lantern stacked on a barrel.

As her eyes adjusted to the dim light, she noticed that several floorboards were pried up, and there appeared to be a very deep hole in the ground beneath them.

She took a step closer, then stopped herself.

"It's all right." Nathaniel motioned for her to continue.

She peered down into the black hole then turned back to Nathaniel. "Am I allowed to inquire what you are doing?"

Nathaniel ran a hand through his hair. "I'm not sure how much David has spoken of the Tea Act . . . ."

"I've read about it myself in the newspaper." Helen couldn't keep a note of irritation from her voice. Did he think her a complete simpleton who had to have the news explained to her?

Nathaniel lowered his eyes. "Of course you've read the paper."

"Is the Tea Act injurious to your business?" she prompted, now grudgingly curious.

"Yes. Well—not precisely. In the past the governor turned a blind eye to smuggled tea, but the Tea Act now allows the East India Company to sell legal English tea without paying any tariffs in London. The governor has been promised a cut of their profits and desires to ensure there is no competition."

"I gather you are in possession of illegal tea you are planning to hide in there." She pointed towards the hole.

"Yes. Exactly."

"Is that not dangerous? I believe the governor announced anyone caught smuggling will be stripped of all land and property."

Nathaniel shrugged. "It might be a little dangerous."

Helen considered him—he didn't appear at all apprehensive at the thought. "I suppose you stand to make a great deal of money?"

"Yes, and David also." Nathaniel learned against the barrel, careful not to bump his lantern.

"David knows of this?"

"He knows about the smuggling but not this cellar. Easier to keep it a secret."

Helen could hardly believe Nathaniel trusted *her* with the knowledge. "I'm a little surprised David is involved in this," she admitted. "That reminds me. The letter—the one I just slid under the door—the money you lent is inside. All of it."

Nathaniel walked over to the door and scooped the letter

off the ground. "I see."

Helen flushed. She hadn't imagined it would be this difficult to tell him she didn't need to see him anymore. "I suppose—well, our business association has come to an end."

Nathaniel shook his head.

"What? All the money is there—all four pounds! Count it if you don't believe me."

"I seem to remember paying for two slices of tart that I've not yet received."

"Oh. I thought you loathed tart." She watched him closely in the dim lantern light.

"To be truthful, I've not much experience with them. I can't remember my mother ever making any, nor any of the cooks aboard any ship I ever sailed on. Most nights I buy my supper at an inn or tavern. It's possible I might like them."

"Well, I'll have to save you some of Verity's, then, for she's the best cook of all of us."

Nathaniel took a deep breath. "I think I should like to try yours." That was a surprise. What had come over him?

"When do you . . . ?" She sought for the right words. "When does the tea . . . ?" She didn't recognize her own voice, which sounded reedy to her own ears.

Nathaniel didn't seem to notice anything amiss. "Friday night."

She made the connection immediately. "The governor's ball!"

"Yes, exactly." Nathaniel smiled at her, and she returned a grin, as if they were co-conspirators.

"I hope you'll be safe."

They stared at each other in the glow of the lantern. Nathaniel took a step closer to her. Helen caught her breath, but a few moments passed, and nothing happened.

"I should probably let you get back to digging."

"May I see you home?"

Helen immediately refused. "Oh, there's no need. I don't want to interrupt your work."

"'Tis no interruption," Nathaniel argued.

Helen stared at him, wondering if he was just trying to be polite. "Very well," she finally accepted. She blinked against the bright afternoon sunlight as he opened the warehouse door. Nathaniel gestured to her to exit first.

She caught him staring at her as they walked. "Is that a new gown?"

Helen glanced down at the red gown peeking beneath her cloak. "Yes, this is new. David insists we mustn't embarrass him by being shabby. I don't mind having new things, of course. I mean, not that wearing something old makes one shabby," she added quickly, glancing sideways at him.

Nathaniel examined his plain black coat. She'd probably offended him.

"What else do you transport?" she asked quickly. "Besides—oh." Helen looked around, but not many people were out on the street. She'd almost said "tea," but she didn't think it was a good idea to draw attention to that in public.

"Spices, mostly. Sometimes fabric. Not silk, ever since David invested in the Pennsylvania silk trade."

"You're a good friend to him."

"He's the best friend I've ever had," Nathaniel replied matter-of-factly. Helen was taken aback. From her observation the men were no more than professional acquaintances. Was there more than she knew to the relationship? Or was Nathaniel bereft of all connections?

"Will you come inside?" Helen offered once they reached her home.

"No, I must return to digging."

He did not wish to prolong their time any further. He was

only being polite in seeing his friend's sister home. "Of course. Thank you for escorting me."

Cassandra was alone in the drawing room when Helen entered. She was flushed from the cold air and distracted by wondering what Nathaniel was thinking.

Cassandra looked up from her embroidery. "Where have you been?"

"Oh, just delivering a letter." Helen busied herself with unfastening her cloak so she didn't have to meet her sister's eyes.

"By yourself?"

"I left by myself." Helen forced herself to meet Cassandra's gaze.

"And returned with Nathaniel Carter?"

Helen glanced at the window. "Were you spying on me?"

"Perhaps."

"Yes, I returned with him. He was polite enough to offer to escort me home." She wasn't sure why she was being evasive, or why her sister's questions made her feel prickly. "Why are you smiling so?"

Cassandra continued to smile down at her embroidery. "I think it a very fine thing."

Helen scoffed. "What, you've decided that I—that he—that we are keeping company together?"

"Are you?" Cassandra asked.

"No!" Helen protested. "One walk and now we are to be married!"

"Perhaps," Cassandra teased.

"You're being ridiculous," Helen muttered, and left the room.

David walked out of his bedroom. "Was that Nathaniel I saw you with just now?"

"Yes," Helen snapped, "I wish you all would find better

ways to occupy your time than spying on me and making conjectures!"

"Conjectures? I don't know what you mean. I don't think he likes you at all."

Helen wasn't sure why this made her feel worse. "What do you know of the matter?"

David snorted. "He's mentioned, more than once, how much *you* dislike *him*."

Helen gaped at him.

David placed a hand on her shoulder. "If you're serious about finding a husband, I'm sure I can line up any number of eligible men."

"How thoughtful." She whirled around and shut her bedroom door firmly.

She slid down the door onto the floor. David and Cassandra were insufferable. She had to leave this place. Perhaps the Hayeses would take her in? She'd been more at ease in Nathaniel's dark warehouse than she was enduring Cassandra's teasing and David's attempts to be helpful.

She was shocked to realize she'd enjoyed Nathaniel's company. He'd spoken openly and trusted her with a secret about his smuggling operation. What if he *did* want to court her?

Of course, he had to dig a cellar, survive a smuggling operation, and manage to escape the law, so thinking that he might actually be interested in courting her was premature to say the least.

She would occupy herself in earning the rest of the money for the society. Whatever happened, she must focus on the tarts and paying off the indenture.

Chapter 9

"Nathaniel!" David called out, waving him over to a table in the coffee room of City Tavern. "Well met." David indicated for Nathaniel to sit across from him. He motioned to a man to bring Nathaniel some coffee. "No tea, I'm afraid."

The servant hurried over to pour coffee and offer a baked good. "Ah, my Sally Lunn bread. Excellent." David scrutinized the contents of a jam jar. "What kind of preserve is this? Not gooseberry, I hope? I've had enough gooseberry to last a lifetime."

"I wasn't certain the city needed another tavern," Nathaniel observed, "but I see the appeal of having such large rooms." He snagged the jam after David set it down.

"Yes, the subscription room provides all the broadsides, journals, and latest news from England, while the bar room provides all the libations a man can stomach. There are some very large meeting rooms upstairs. Large enough to hold a ball, so I understand, which has brought great joy to my household."

Nathaniel snorted. “A strong endorsement. Are you trying to get me to invest in this place?”

“No, though I wish I had done so myself.”

Nathaniel tried to spread jam—raspberry—on his bread without allowing the knife to touch the blisters on his hands. He was no stranger to hard work and had many calluses, but shoveling twelve hours a day had taken a toll on him.

David leaned forward conspiratorially. “Have you secured a location for the, er, cargo?”

“I have.”

“Very well.” David kept his voice lowered, though the two other tables seemed engrossed in their own conversations. “I’ll escort Cassandra and Helen to the governor’s ball, then give some pretense for leaving after securing another ride home for the ladies. Being seen at the ball will give me the perfect alibi should anyone question my involvement.”

“Are you still invited to the ball after that argument you had with Winthrop?”

David smirked. “Nothing short of my being convicted of murder would keep them from inviting the son of an English marquess to their ball. I lend them consequence!”

“And Helen doesn’t mind attending after all that’s transpired with Winthrop?” Nathaniel hoped he sounded casual. He didn’t want David discovering that he thought of Helen all the time.

“Blast Winthrop! I’ve been witness to such drama as even Shakespeare couldn’t conceive. My wife’s cousin Temperance boasted to all in her acquaintance that Winthrop asked her to open the ball with him, so Helen has been in agony trying to decide if she should tell Temperance of Winthrop’s perfidy with the taxes.”

This was far too much trouble over a small matter. Couldn’t Helen enlighten her cousin and be done with it?

"I envy you, Nathaniel, I really do, for traversing the Delaware with the rankest thieves couldn't possibly be more dangerous than the pit of lions I'll be dropped into on Friday evening."

He chuckled. "Surely it can't be that bad?"

"Ha! Again you reveal your ignorance of women. I've tried to guide Helen so that she doesn't cause offense to her aunt and uncle, but she refuses to see reason."

Nathaniel frowned. Helen didn't seem to appreciate any meddling in her affairs.

David shifted back in his chair. "This will amuse you. Cassandra firmly believes that you harbor a tendre for Helen. Apparently she took your escorting Helen the other night as evidence you mean to court her. Ridiculous, is it not? I told her that you could barely tolerate her sister."

Nathaniel chuckled woodenly. "Ridiculous," he agreed. Had David also told Helen that? His stomach twisted.

All around them men started to stand.

"Ah, 'tis time for the Sons of Liberty meeting." David pushed away from the table. "Would you care to attend?"

"Is that why you asked me here?"

"We are to draft a notice to the captain of the *Polly* that he'll be greeted by the Tar and Feather Committee if he tries to dock in Philadelphia."

"I'll believe it when I witness it with my own eyes," Nathaniel retorted, standing up to leave. "I've more preparations to make."

David followed him out into the corridor.

"Good evening, Beaufort!" Nathaniel recognized Dr. Benjamin Rush.

"Good evening, Dr. Rush," David rejoined, following his friend upstairs to the meeting.

Nathaniel slipped outside into the cold night.

"Sir, will you buy my last paper?" a boy called.

Taking pity on him, Nathaniel tossed the boy a ha'penny. He turned the paper in his blistered hands, remembering how Helen admonished him for assuming she only garnered the news from David.

He wasn't sure why he didn't want David to know that he was interested in Helen. He felt protective of the knowledge and a bit embarrassed. How would he bring it up? Men didn't go around talking to other men about their feelings!

He could take the paper to Helen to show he valued her intelligence. David wasn't at home, so he wouldn't have to know about it. Nathaniel wasn't sure how things were normally done in courting. Was a newspaper an acceptable offering? *Was* he courting her?

His heart hammered as he approached the door to Josiah Hayes's law office. This was ridiculous. He might not know much about women, but he was certain men didn't make a gift of a newspaper to young ladies they were interested in courting.

He was about to turn away and walk home when the window above him opened.

"Coming in?" Cassandra called down to him.

"Uh, yes, I was just—um, is David home?" He winced. For all he knew, David told her he was going to meet Nathaniel and now he seemed like an idiot.

"No, but do come up and get warm for a moment."

"I thank you. I—" Nathaniel searched for something to say. He didn't know what he'd even say to Helen if she was even at home.

The door in front of him swung open. Helen, covered in a dusting of flour, was standing on the threshold.

"Good evening. Coming up?" Her welcoming smile reassured him.

"Just for a moment," he managed, following her up the stairs.

Helen glanced down. "What's in the paper?"

"I'm not sure. I brought it for you." He thrust the paper at her, hoping she remembered their conversation at the warehouse.

"Oh! Thank you."

Cassandra stood at the top of the stairs. "Come into the kitchen," she bade him. "It's the warmest room in the house with both fires going."

Nathaniel didn't have much experience of cookery, but it was evident when he entered the kitchen that Helen was in the midst of making more tarts.

Helen noticed the direction of his gaze. "I'm improving. I can now make something even our cook finds edible and manage not to wreck the kitchen in the process."

Cassandra didn't follow them into the kitchen. "How do things proceed?" Helen asked, resuming her work.

"Very well. I'm making progress on . . . my endeavor."

"Oh, could you give me that jar there—My! What's happened to your hands?" Helen grabbed his right hand and peered at the blisters there. "These are awful! All from shoveling, I suppose? Sit there."

She retrieved a large stone basin with some difficulty, refusing Nathaniel's assistance. He sat as bid, not wanting to incur her wrath. Helen poured some water out of a bucket to fill the basin and then added a few drops of something else.

"Essence of lavender," she explained. "It works to soothe burns, so I imagine it will work quite well on blisters."

Nathaniel plunged his hands into the water.

"Well?"

The cool water was pleasant. "Very nice."

Helen returned his smile and resumed working once more.

She was beautiful in the flickering light of the fire. If family life meant being warm and comfortable and having a beautiful woman take care of him, he would very much like to have a family.

"I think even I'm heartily sick of gooseberry by now," she admitted, "though I should never reveal that to David. He tells me I should throw the unsold tarts directly in the rubbish heap and swears he will eat no more, but it seems so wasteful to do so."

"Is there—might I try some?" Nathaniel stumbled over the words. He was turning into a fool. He never tripped over his speech in business.

"Of course. You should be doing us a great service! Perhaps you will not find it too sweet after all." She cut him a slice and brought the plate to him. He made to take his hands out of the water.

"Oh no—leave them. Here." Helen picked up the slice and brought it to his mouth. Nathaniel bit down carefully and chewed slowly, savoring the taste. It was a little tart, but pleasingly sweet at the same time.

Helen watched him. He hastened to swallow. "Very good," he assured her.

Helen blushed prettily and lifted the tart again. Nathaniel's breath caught.

The door of the kitchen opened behind them.

"What the devil is going on here?" David stood in the doorway. Nathaniel jumped up, splashing water everywhere.

"I was just—"

"You're home early." Helen placed the tart slice back on the plate. "Nathaniel was doing you a service by finishing the tart you find so repulsive."

David's eyes narrowed.

Nathaniel shook the water off his hands. "I should be

leaving. Thank you for the tart and the water. Good night."

David followed him downstairs. "Do you mind telling me what that was really about?" he asked.

Nathaniel scratched his ear uncomfortably. "I was just walking by, and Cassandra asked me to warm myself by the fire."

"You don't live anywhere near here," David retorted. "And you told me you had more preparations to attend to."

Nathaniel shrugged, unable to think of anything else to say.

"Well, if you do intend to court my sister-in-law—and I find it a very shocking thing if you do, for you appeared to roundly loathe each other a few days ago—you must go through me!"

"Of course!" This must be one of the rules of courtship he knew so little about.

"Fine. Good night." David turned and went inside.

Nathaniel shoved his hands into his pockets. The memory of the cool water on his hands was pleasant, but Helen's kindness warmed him throughout. He would ask David's permission to court her when this was all over, he decided, no matter how awkward it might make things. The thought of having a kitchen like that to sit in every evening, along with Helen to talk to, was an inducement that outweighed any cost.

Chapter 10

For the first time since beginning the tart scheme Helen dreaded going to the market. She would see Temperance for the first time since deciding it was her Christian duty to tell her cousin the truth about Winthrop.

Perhaps Temperance wouldn't listen, but Helen felt she had to tell her about the false tax he levied. Temperance continued to allude to her upcoming marriage to him, and Helen would feel terrible if her cousin entered into such a commitment without knowing his true nature.

She forced herself to walk into the baker's stall. Jane was already laying out tarts while Temperance waved at potential customers.

"Oh, Helen!" Temperance rushed to embrace her. "I'm so happy you're here! I want to hear all about the gown you're wearing to the ball." Helen felt a twinge of guilt for what she had to say to her cousin.

"What are you wearing to the ball?" she asked, trying to make polite conversation before delving into a more difficult subject.

Temperance launched into a detailed account of the elaborate gown she had commissioned from French fashion plates. "And a ribbon to cross over the bodice," she finally finished. "What about you?" she asked Jane.

"I'm not attending," Jane informed them.

"I'm sorry," Temperance said, patting Jane's hand sympathetically. Helen wasn't sure Jane actually mourned not being included.

"Well, we have nearly twenty pounds," Helen announced after counting what they had taken in so far, refraining from adding that it was no thanks to Winthrop's interference. "Surely that will be enough to purchase the indenture."

Jane shook her head. "I'm afraid not. The family has heard rumors about what we are trying to do and feel they can ask for much more. They want forty pounds."

Helen's mouth dropped open. "That's beyond belief! Forty pounds is what an adult indenture would cost. You must negotiate with them!"

"I fear doing so will only give them cause to raise the price further. They will assume young ladies with wealthy parents have access to unlimited funds."

"Surely not!" Helen argued. "It's because some of our relatives are so influential that they will be likely to appease us. I'm certain Uncle Josiah will help us!"

Helen and Jane looked over at Temperance, who shrugged. "Perhaps."

"We must try to raise the rest of the money they ask," Jane insisted. "The situation is growing worse for Mary."

An idea came to Helen. "You said this family lives next to yours?"

Jane nodded.

Helen turned to Temperance. "Do they have any connection to Uncle Josiah which he could use in our favor?"

"Mr. Franklin Morris?" Jane supplied.

"I don't know all of Father's clients. I know his most important client, however—Governor Morley. And I'm to open the ball with his son tomorrow night!" She clasped both hands to her chest with an expression of ecstasy Helen found almost painful to witness.

"Temperance," Helen began, stomach twisting. Temperance was the unspoken leader of all their friends *and* her cousin. If Helen offended her, she might also offend her aunt and uncle. "Are you aware that Winthrop has been stealing money from us daily?"

Temperance crossed her arms. "I heard he appropriates a legal tax."

Helen frowned. "No, David insists it's not legal. Winthrop's invented the whole thing to steal from us."

Temperance gasped. "How dare you accuse Winthrop of theft as if he were nothing more than a petty criminal! *You* are the guilty one."

Helen was determined not to lose her composure and reminded herself that it was natural for Temperance to have a hard time hearing criticism about Winthrop. "Guilty of what, pray tell?" she asked, as calmly as she was able to manage.

"*You* are disloyal to your king by trying to avoid lawful taxation! It's treason!" Temperance pointed a finger at Helen.

Jane looked as if she would try to intercede, but Helen ignored her. She couldn't remember why she must remain calm.

She drew herself up to her full height and placed a hand on her hip. "Cousin, need I remind you that *I* was born in England while *you* have never once set foot upon its shores? I beg you to recall that before accusing me of treachery to a king you haven't been anywhere near."

Temperance gasped. "I refuse to stay here another moment to be insulted in such a manner." She stormed out of the booth.

That hadn't gone very well. Temperance already knew about the tax. Helen's interference had been superfluous.

"You tried," Jane whispered, squeezing Helen's hand.

Helen had a hard time focusing on the tart sales throughout the day. After she gave a third customer the wrong change, Jane assured Helen she could finish out the day and encouraged her to go home and finalize her preparations for the ball.

She had no plan to primp for hours to impress anyone, since she knew Nathaniel wouldn't be there. He'd surprised her with the newspaper and his enjoyment of tart. It would be foolish to pretend she didn't want him to court her when he occupied her thoughts constantly.

She did her best to focus on the matter at hand and walked briskly across town to Jane's home. She intended to settle the matter of the indenture with the Morris family, for even if she could not convince Temperance to cast off Winthrop, she was certain she could resolve this. After all, her plans had been successful at raising an enormous sum. Just that morning David had admitted he hadn't expected them to be able to purchase the indenture.

Helen looked at the row of houses and recognized Jane's at once from previous visits. Choosing at random, she knocked at the door to the right, feeling it had a more sinister aspect.

"I'm here to see Mrs. Morris," she announced to a servant.

The maid, taking in the fine quality of Helen's clothing, gave her a polite curtsy. "You'll be wanting down that way." She thumbed at the house on the other side. Helen hoped Jane's family was not observing her through the windows.

"I am here to see Mrs. Morris," she repeated at the correct

house. A young boy let her in.

"Ma!" he screamed. "Lady to see you!"

Helen waited several minutes for the lady of the house. "Good afternoon," she greeted when Mrs. Morris finally appeared. "I am Miss Helen Crofton. I realize this visit is unannounced, but I've a proposition to make to you."

Mrs. Morris scrutinized Helen while Helen did the same to her hostess. She was a middle-aged woman dressed in the style of a much younger woman—many flounces and bows and a lace cap with a large red ribbon.

"Perhaps you know my uncle, Josiah Hayes?" Helen prompted after a few moments' uncomfortable silence.

"Follow me."

That did it. Once again, Helen's instincts had led her to accurately predict what would impress Mrs. Morris.

Helen entered a small, overwrought drawing room stuffed with all manner of plates, badly painted landscapes, and embroidered cushions. It could have passed as a shop selling tasteless decorations.

"Make yourself comfortable, Miss Crofton." Mrs. Morris pointed to a chair. "I've a notion of what brings you here."

"Very good. Is the young lady—is she here?"

Mrs. Morris inclined her head. "She's just upstairs, sewing. We've taken many such young girls out of Christian charity. They need a woman to watch over them. I shudder to think where some young girls end up when they make that precarious journey from England!"

Helen reminded herself she must be polite at all costs, though she badly wanted to tell Mrs. Morris that she knew the goings-on here were far less than Christian in nature.

She took a deep breath and began. "I'm a member of a charitable society. It's our mission—" She broke off, trying to consider how to word this delicately. "We'd like to offer opportunities to young girls to break their indentures and learn a useful trade. One of our members has put forward the name of your servant as a likely candidate. Of course, we would reimburse you for the remainder of her indenture."

Mrs. Morris shook her head sadly. "I'm afraid we have gotten too attached to Mary to give her up. She's become like another member of the family."

Helen's smile fell. It was time to get serious. "Mrs. Morris, I understand from a very trustworthy source that Mary isn't entirely happy here. Maybe you aren't aware that one of your sons has been harassing her?"

Mrs. Morris's eyes narrowed. "That is a falsehood. I will call for her and let her tell you herself. Mary!" The woman went to the door and called in a loud voice.

A young girl quickly descended the stairs. She was very pretty, Helen noticed, but still had the look of a child.

"Mary, someone has been spreading rumors that you are unhappy here. Is this true?" Mrs. Morris demanded.

Mary stared at the floor. "No, ma'am."

"Do you know who started these rumors?"

"No, ma'am." Mary wouldn't look up.

"Has Mr. Jack bothered you?"

"No, ma'am," Mary whispered, barely audible.

Mrs. Morris raised an eyebrow at Helen. "Are you satisfied?"

Helen was not sure what to say. She wasn't, but she didn't know what else she could do. She nodded tightly.

"Very well. Mary, be off. Now," Mrs. Morris said, turning back to Helen, "I don't know why you, a stranger, should be so impertinent as to come here and insult me based on unsubstantiated rumor!"

Helen took another deep breath. "I'm sorry. I must have misunderstood. Still, our society would very much like to proceed. We could compensate you as much as twenty pounds for the inconvenience of giving up your servant."

"Out of the question."

Helen's spirits fell. Had all their work been for naught? Jane should have been more certain the Morrises would give in when she set them on this path.

"I couldn't think of letting her go for less than forty pounds," Mrs. Morris continued, "So that I might cover the wages of a hired girl until another servant can be found who satisfies our requirements."

Helen gaped at her audacity—to pretend she cared for Mary and then to ask for so much money. "A hired girl's wages can be no more than four pounds for an entire year!"

"I don't expect a young, unmarried lady such as yourself to understand household affairs." Mrs. Morris cocked her head and smirked. "Well, perhaps not so very young." She shook out her overly ruffled underskirt.

Helen ignored the barb. It would not do to reflect too much on the insults of a mature lady who dressed like an ill-favored spinster attempting to nab a husband. "There's no way our society can pay that much."

"That's a pity. Perhaps you can find a few benefactors?"

Helen glared at her.

"No? Well, if you change your mind, you know where to return." Mrs. Morris stood and gestured towards the door. "Oh, and Miss Crofton? I should hate to hear any more of these rumors. My husband owns this row of buildings, did you know? If I found out that any of my neighbors were involved with spreading vicious rumors about my family, I would certainly have to ask him to evict the troublemakers. Good day."

Helen stormed down the street and marched towards the apartment. Mrs. Morris was the most odious woman Helen had ever encountered.

What would happen to Mary now? Jane had attempted to warn Helen about Mrs. Morris's nature, but she'd been certain she knew best how to handle the situation. Now she'd ruined the society's chance to help Mary. She just *knew* Mary had been lying when Mrs. Morris questioned her. It was clear the girl was terrified!

Jane and her family might also suffer as a result of Helen's actions. She felt as if lead coated the inside of her stomach. Every step was heavy. How could she possibly face everyone from the society?

She was so distracted that she walked into someone and nearly lost her balance. Hands seized her arms and steadied her. Helen looked up at her rescuer—and found Nathaniel looking back at her.

"I'm sorry," she stammered. Had she conjured him out of her mind? He was standing right in front of her home.

Nathaniel grinned at her. "Lost in thought? Pondering your tart empire?"

She returned a half smile. "No, nothing so grand. Are you coming up?"

"Yes, I have business with David."

"At least you have his permission to be here this time," she teased.

Nathaniel followed her up the narrow stars, and Helen led him to the dining room where David had started working when his study became Helen's bedroom.

She would *not* interfere with their business. She had many other things to occupy her and no time to make a fool of herself over Nathaniel by barging in on his meeting. If she happened to settle herself in the drawing room where it would be impossible to miss his walking by when he left, that was just a coincidence. She needed to focus her mind on how to free Mary.

She would hate for Nathaniel to mistakenly think she was waiting for him. She rummaged in Cassandra's work cabinet and pulled out some embroidery she'd never gotten around to finishing.

She'd barely set to work before Cassandra came into the room and eyed the cushion Helen was stitching. "I haven't seen that in ages."

"I've been intending to finish it for some time now, but the tarts have kept me occupied." Was that the sound of a door opening?

"I think you started that when David and I were first married," Cassandra persisted. "I forgot it entirely! I wonder that you should bring it out now."

"You think too much on it," Helen insisted. "I need something to occupy my mind."

Cassandra smirked. "Too much weighing on you of late? Perhaps a certain captain is to blame?"

"Cassandra!" Helen hissed. "He's in the other room with David! He'll hear you!"

They heard footsteps in the hallway. Nathaniel stopped in the doorway and bowed. He motioned to her embroidery. "Is that for the stand? Planning to sell . . . whatever that is?"

"Are you interested in purchasing?" Cassandra inquired.

Nathaniel froze.

"She's teasing," Helen explained. "This isn't for sale—it's a cushion I have meant to make David a present of for three years now."

Nathaniel stepped further into the room.

"Oh, I forgot!" Cassandra jumped up. "Excuse me! I must speak to Peggy."

Helen tried to ignore her racing heart. "Would you care to take a seat?"

Nathaniel took a seat next to her on the couch.

"How is—" Helen began.

"I understand—" Nathaniel started to say. They laughed. "Go ahead," he encouraged her.

"How is the cellar?"

Nathaniel flexed his hands. "It's finished."

She lowered her voice. "Then all is well—for the *plan*?"

"Everything is in order," Nathaniel assured her.

"Are you scared?"

Nathaniel waved a hand. "It's nothing. I'll be home early." If he was that sure, it must truly be safe.

Helen leaned closer. "I hope all goes well tomorrow night."

Nathaniel stretched one arm out over the back of the couch. "You'll be at the ball tomorrow night."

"I wish I didn't have to." She looked down at her embroidery and realized she'd pulled the needle through in the wrong place.

"Are you not fond of dancing?" He sounded almost hopeful.

"I'm very fond of dancing, just not attending balls with idiots like Winthrop Morley."

"Oh. Yes, he is insufferable." Nathaniel ran a finger across the initials she'd already stitched onto the cushion cover.

"I wish some ill might befall him so that he would be forced to stop collecting his false tax." Helen stabbed the needle into her embroidery.

Nathaniel placed a hand over hers. "Are you sure you're well?"

Helen's eyes welled up with tears. "No," she whispered. Because of her, Mary would stay trapped with the Morrises and Jane might be thrown out of her home.

Nathaniel swallowed. "Do you wish to talk about it?"

Helen began to explain everything when David strode into

the room and collapsed on the couch. Nathaniel snatched his hand back. Where was Cassandra? Helen had been certain speaking to Peggy was all a ruse to leave the two of them alone for a little while. Couldn't she have occupied David as well?

"I thought you were leaving," David said. "Important matters to attend to and all that."

"I'm not in such a great hurry that I can't stop to speak a few words to a lady."

David snorted. "Oh, don't let *me* stop you!"

Nathaniel turned back to Helen, who found she did not want to discuss the matter of Mary and Mrs. Morris in front of David.

Still, Nathaniel gazed at her expectantly.

"I had a fight with my cousin." This was safer.

"Ha! I told you not to speak to her!" David taunted.

Helen glared at him. "I doubt you could have remained silent at her professions of undying love for that cretin, Winthrop."

"Of course not," David agreed. "But I also wouldn't work myself into a passion about it afterwards."

"You see what I have to put up with?" she whispered to Nathaniel.

Nathaniel grinned at her. "I'm sorry—can things be mended between you?"

"I'm not sure. Perhaps she will come to her senses and see that Winthrop is horrid."

Nathaniel glanced at David, who had somehow produced a penknife to twirl. "Well, I must go."

"I'll walk you to the door."

David stood in the doorway and watched.

"Perhaps—" Nathaniel began hesitantly. "Perhaps Sunday you might accompany me for a walk in North Square?"

"I would like that," Helen replied, pointedly ignoring David's scowls.

Nathaniel bowed to her. "Good night."

"What was that all about?" Helen rounded on David the moment Nathaniel left.

"He really should ask me if he can escort you anywhere. And you're not to be alone with him again!"

Helen gaped at him. "You are medieval! Do you mean to lock me in a tower?"

"Do you know of any? Cassandra and I would visit you. We could do with an outing."

Helen stormed past him into her bedroom. She would have told Nathaniel about Mrs. Morris, she realized, even though it revealed what a complete fool she was. For whatever reason, she felt he would not think the worst of her if he knew. How had that happened? Not long ago she thought he loathed her roundly and now—well, she wasn't sure exactly how he felt, but he certainly seemed as if he wanted to court her.

The thought filled her with a warmth even the memory of her great failure couldn't dispel. There was a kindness to him she hadn't ever seen before. Had it always been there and she'd failed to notice it? She had to admit to herself that she would be severely disappointed if he didn't want to court her after all. She was even beginning to think that she might enjoy being a merchant's wife.

No, she admitted to herself—Nathaniel's wife.

Chapter 11

Helen thought her party was dressed well enough to appear at a royal ball rather than merely at the governor of Pennsylvania's. She wore a green silk *robe à la française* with a gold petticoat layered with ruffles and a pair of full lace cuffs, while Cassandra and David coordinated in blue. It was a little nauseating that they always liked to match at parties, but they seemed to enjoy it immensely. At least if she married Nathaniel, she would never fear him matching her unless she dressed in unrelieved black.

They promenaded down one side of the ballroom after being announced. David immediately secured Cassandra a seat, though she insisted she felt fresh and ready to dance. Helen listened to them debate the merits of Cassandra's dancing in her pregnant state until she could not bear it any longer and left to find someone else to speak to.

Her cousin Patience tapped her foot impatiently from a chair in a far corner.

"Planning to dance?" Helen asked.

"I was dragged here against my will. Papa thinks I'll be a

steadying influence on Temperance, but that's a lost cause."

Helen turned to observe Temperance and Winthrop on the dance floor. Their expressions and manners were so stately and exaggerated they might have been on the stage.

Out of the corner of her eye she saw David approaching his old friend Dr. Benjamin Rush. Helen laughed to herself. David had transformed from someone terrified of a hint of pox to a man who couldn't resist discussing the latest medical discoveries.

A young man approached Patience and asked her to dance. Apparently she felt she mustn't refuse him and ended up being dragged into a reel.

Helen took the chair Patience vacated and amused herself by watching all her acquaintances. Euphemia, dressed and powdered to the peak of fashion, laughed with her dance partner. Constance stumbled over the steps as she day-dreamed.

She must distract herself from worrying about Nathaniel. He'd assured her he was quite safe.

Helen saw David break away from Dr. Rush and approach Cassandra, who seemed startled by whatever he said to her. He then turned and left the ballroom with so furtive an expression Helen was instantly suspicious and leapt out of her seat to follow him.

A footman was helping David into his cloak.

"You're leaving?" she demanded.

"Dr. Rush has just informed me of a very pressing matter I must attend to," he replied, not meeting her eyes. "He'll escort you and Cassandra home."

"Wait. What errand would the doctor send you on at the beginning of a ball?"

"Something for—" He lowered his voice. "—the Sons of Liberty." He raised his eyebrows as if he'd told her something very secretive—as if he didn't bandy his association with the group at every opportunity.

Helen huffed. "You're going to assist Nathaniel!"

David immediately refuted this. "No. Nothing like that."

"I know you are, for I cannot imagine anything else that would drag you away from this party after half an hour. I should've known you were up to something when you wore the same suit of clothing you wore to the Harrisons' ball. Oh well, enjoy playing at smuggling."

"Keep your voice down," David hissed, looking around. The footman who brought his cloak had already disappeared. "Don't breathe a word of this to *anyone*. Not even Cassandra! The more who know about it, the more likely it is we will be caught and punished."

Helen snorted. "Nathaniel said it was perfectly harmless."

"He lied. We are in great danger of losing everything. Who knows? The constable might show up and shoot at us!" David seemed very improperly excited at this prospect.

"What? And this is how you care for my sister—rushing off into the night to put your life in danger when she carries your child?" She crossed her arms.

"I'm doing this *for* Cassandra! I mean to buy her the home she deserves. Now, I must go. Do not tell anyone of this!"

Helen stared after him. Was David imagining more danger in the business because he found it thrilling, or was there really such risk?

Well, she certainly would tell Cassandra. If a man put his life in danger, his wife certainly had a right to know. Her sister was standing by the door when Helen reentered the ballroom.

"Come outside for a moment," Helen bade Cassandra, slipping an arm through hers.

"Did David tell you he had to leave on some errand?" Cassandra whispered.

"Yes, that is what I wish to speak of." She waited until they were safely outside and made sure no one was around to overhear. "David has gone to assist Nathaniel with a smuggling operation!"

"He told you this?"

"I guessed it. I knew Nathaniel was bringing some illegal tea in tonight, and when David left so suddenly . . . . Should we prevent it?"

Cassandra shook her head. "The smuggling? Oh, no. Let's pretend as if nothing is wrong. David probably does not want his absence noted."

"You said there would be dancing bears out here?" Euphemia's voice broke into their conversation.

Helen whirled around to Eugenia standing with Winthrop, who wore a half smile.

"The bears?" Euphemia repeated.

"I must have been wrong. I'll take you back inside." Had he heard them? Surely not—she'd checked, and no one was around.

"But Winthrop, you said—"

His words were slurred, as if he'd had too much punch. "Back inside! Perhaps a nice cup of tea will set you to rights."

A chill went through her. Why had he mentioned tea?

"Come, let's return also," Cassandra urged her. "Not a word," she admonished. "We must act as if all is well."

When they returned to the ballroom, Winthrop had disappeared.

A coincidence, Helen tried to reassure herself. He would reappear shortly, as ridiculous as ever. Even if he had heard her, he was probably too drunk to make sense of what she'd said. At least, she hoped so.

Nathaniel's heart pounded as he navigated a rowboat loaded with illegal tea around a particularly sharp bend in the Delaware River. Unloading the tea onto the rowboats had been easy. Nobody in Chester, where he had temporarily berthed the *Good King George*, raised an eye. Goods went up the river to Philadelphia all the time—and nighttime trips were not infrequent.

Matlack's crew was as loathsome as the man himself, so Nathaniel was glad he wouldn't have a reason to deal with them after this was all over. They just needed to make it to the dock, unload the tea, and haul it to Nathaniel's warehouse cellar, then he would pay them and hopefully never see them again.

Cruising a river on a rowboat was a fair bit harder than steering while his larger ship was towed in, and his hands were still raw from digging. Still, it felt good to draw so near to the end of the business.

As the rowboat rounded the bend Nathaniel could make out a tiny pinprick of light. He squinted—was he missing the second light? He drew a little closer and realized there was only one lit lantern—the sign for trouble. With only one light, the tea could not be unloaded and would have to be dumped in the river.

The smuggling crew knew its business. With barely a sound, tea chests were lowered into the water and released. With a small huff, Nathaniel cut the ropes holding the eight chests his boat carried and tipped them into the river. So much for the plan.

The light of a half moon allowed him to see the others turn back downriver. He should do the same. He'd agreed on the plan with Matlack.

What had gone wrong? Although he couldn't see him, Nathaniel knew David was standing on the dock. He'd risked everything to help Nathaniel—and he couldn't abandon him now. He navigated to a pier further down than the one David stood on, dipping his oar carefully to avoid making a sound.

He tied off the boat and pulled himself silently onto the pier then walked carefully towards David. At first he couldn't see what was wrong, but as he drew nearer, he realized another man was standing nearby.

The grating voice of Winthrop Morley pierced through the air. "I dare not catch a chill by waiting out here any longer. You'll have to come alone." He was drunk enough to slur his words.

"Very well; it appears my friend is not coming."

Nathaniel reacted without thinking and stepped forward into the light cast by David's lantern. "Sorry I'm late."

"I thought you'd never come," David drawled, lowering the lantern a little.

Winthrop turned and pointed a pistol at Nathaniel, who threw his arms in the air to stop the fool from firing on him. Winthrop smirked. "I knew I'd find you here. A rat can never escape a trap."

Nathaniel ignored this jibe. "I'd feel more at ease if you put the gun down. I didn't know you'd invited him," he added to David, who shrugged.

"I have your lady friend to thank for leading me straight to you! You should never have trusted a woman with important business," Winthrop admonished

Nathaniel didn't believe him. Unless David told Cassandra, the only lady he knew who was aware of the plan tonight was Helen. She would never have told.

"My father has been eager to apprehend you ever since

we learned of your plans to smuggle illegal goods into the city. Imagine how proud he'll be of me when I bring you to him! If you would just call your men in so they can unload my cargo?"

"What men? I'm here to meet Mr. Beaufort so we might take the night air." Nathaniel flinched. The smell of the docks off the river wasn't particularly pleasant.

Winthrop took a step forward. "Don't lie to me. Where's the tea?"

"What tea?" Nathaniel feigned innocence.

Winthrop growled and advanced towards Nathaniel, stumbling from intoxication. Nathaniel winced, hoping Winthrop wouldn't accidentally set the pistol off. "I know you're bringing in illegal tea in defiance of my father's order. What else would bring you out here at this time of night? Nobody would take the air here! It's probably rolling with miasmas."

David shuddered violently and lifted his free hand to cover his nose and mouth.

Nathaniel shrugged, hands still in the air. "I'm used to the smell after so many years at sea."

"It's no matter. My father will take my word over yours any day. Now, walk slowly towards him," Winthrop said, waving his pistol at David.

"I also have powerful friends," David attempted. "If you let us go, we can all meet with your father tomorrow and settle this as gentlemen."

"We shall settle it with him tonight. He thinks I've no proper occupation, but I'll show my worth." He laughed, the ridiculous sound incongruous with the seriousness of the situation.

"I really must insist. My wife will be worried if I'm not at home."

Nathaniel felt ill. He didn't think Winthrop was a threat to them, as long as he didn't accidently fire off that pistol. He was also nearly certain the governor would not arrest them with no evidence of wrongdoing, if only due to David's lofty position. However, he felt terrible about worrying Cassandra and Helen.

"Morley—" Nathaniel began. Maybe he could talk Winthrop into letting David go.

Winthrop whipped around. "You are worthless!" he spat. He lunged forward and stuck the barrel of the pistol in Nathaniel's face.

Nathaniel's hands shot out to move the barrel upwards and away from himself. He tried to get the weapon away, but Winthrop only squirmed and twisted, so he wasn't able to pry it away.

Suddenly a shot rang out, and Winthrop fell to the ground. David stood over him with the lantern raised in the air. Half the glass was shattered, and the flame sputtered and danced.

Nathaniel tried to catch his breath, mind racing to make sense of what happened. "You struck him?"

"Yes, are you all right?" David crouched down to examine Winthrop.

"He missed." Nathaniel patted his chest to be sure.

"Winthrop breathes." David sounded relieved.

"You should go," Nathaniel encouraged. "That shot might draw attention. I'll see him safe."

"It will be hard for you to move him."

Nathaniel tried to focus his thoughts. "He must have conveyance nearby."

In mute agreement they set off together, leaving Winthrop on the dock. His coach was easy to find with his family crest painted on the door.

"Your master is unwell," David called. "We require your assistance to move him."

Winthrop's coachman looped his horse's reins and

climbed down to them. While David held the light, Nathaniel and the coachman managed to half-carry, half-drag Winthrop to the coach and heft him inside.

"You'll see him home?" David asked.

"Aye," the coachman called, snapping the reins and moving the carriage forward.

David turned. "I must away, and quickly. Come, walk with me; I sent my coach back already." He walked faster than Nathaniel had seen him do before.

They reached Nathaniel's street first. "Thank you," Nathaniel said, the words inadequate for all David had done for him.

"Yes, of course. I'll come see you tomorrow." David hurried off down the road, carrying the broken lantern.

Nathaniel walked slowly towards his home, going over everything that happened and wondering if he could have done something different. Winthrop took an almost unnatural delight in thwarting him.

He was certain he wouldn't sleep well, but to his surprise, he had barely laid his head upon his pillow before drifting off.

Chapter 12

It was after four in the morning by the time Helen and Cassandra returned home from the ball. They'd both been too tense to enjoy the party, but they didn't want to draw any attention to David's absence by leaving early. Finally, Dr. Rush professed his desire to leave, and they readily agreed.

"David?" Cassandra called as they entered the apartment. There was no answer. "David?" she tried again.

"He's not here." Westing emerged from the kitchen. "He asked me to wait here tonight until he returned, though he thought that would not be long after midnight. He sent the coach back without him."

"Oh dear." Cassandra steadied herself against the corridor.

"I'll go search for him," Westing said, starting off immediately.

"Where did the coach drop him?" Cassandra demanded.

Westing turned back. "I don't know; I'll try and rouse the coachman."

"The docks," Helen suggested. Westing nodded.

Cassandra stared after Westing. "What could've happened to David?"

Helen placed a hand on her sister's arm. "Perhaps it's taking longer than they expected to move the cargo. Come, you should change out of those things."

She led her sister into her bedroom and helped her undress like she had when they were children. Helen suggested Cassandra lie down, but this was met by a glare, so Helen knew it was a lost cause.

"Give me that," Cassandra said, reaching for David's wrapper. She slid her arms in and cinched the belt around her waist. They sat in the drawing room until the sun started to rise, but there was no sign of David or Westing.

"Perhaps Westing is assisting David?" Helen suggested.

Cassandra buried her face in her hands. Helen felt she could sit still no longer.

"I'll be back soon," she said, rushing from the room.

Nathaniel woke to the sound of someone pounding on his door. It was unlike David to be such an early riser.

"What?" he called through the door.

"It's me—Helen."

Nathaniel sat up. Something must be terribly wrong for her to show up at his home. He hastened to pull on his clothing and opened his door. "What's happened?"

Helen looked as if she'd no sleep at all, and she was still dressed in an elaborate gown. "It's David. He never came back."

"Never came back?" Nathaniel repeated. That made no sense. He remembered what Winthrop said—someone, a woman, had told him where to find Nathaniel. He shook his head to dislodge the thought, irrelevant at this moment. Of course Helen hadn't told Winthrop anything. He hurried to fasten the rest of the buttons on his waistcoat.

"Was he involved in the smuggling?" Helen demanded.

Nathaniel shoved his arms through his coat sleeves. "He was, but he should have been home hours ago."

"We were back at four, and his valet said he'd never seen him."

Nathaniel ran a hand through his hair. "I—I will accompany you home, and then I'll go out and look for him. Perhaps he—I don't know."

The cobbler who rented Nathaniel the room was occupied with a customer as Helen and Nathaniel descended the stairs from Nathaniel's apartment. Nathaniel was glad of this, and especially glad the cobbler's nosy wife wasn't present. She would have done more than raise an eyebrow to see Helen leaving his room.

"How did you know where I live?" Nathaniel asked.

"I went to your warehouse," Helen explained, "and while you obviously weren't there, I asked a man entering the next building if he knew you and he did. He directed me to your address. A large man, rather bald," she added.

"Foster," Nathaniel said quickly. Mr. Foster owned the warehouse across from Nathaniel's. He was relieved Helen hadn't run into one of the more unsavory characters who sometimes hung about the street.

They hastened through the Philadelphia streets in the dawn light. Nathaniel scanned their route as he considered where David could possibly have gone.

The door to the Beauforts' apartment was ajar when they entered the main floor. Josiah Hayes was sitting across from Cassandra, who sat by the drawing room fire wearing a man's dressing gown. Westing hovered nearby.

Helen ran to her sister. "What is it?" Cassandra didn't answer.

"I received a missive this morning from David," Hayes explained. "He was taken into custody late last night."

Nathaniel drew in a sharp breath. "For what?"

Hayes cleared his throat. "Murder."

Helen jumped up. "What!" she exclaimed. "Who's died?"

"Winthrop Morley." Hayes's voice was grave.

Nathaniel gripped the cabinet next to him for balance. Winthrop couldn't have died.

"I don't know much more," Hayes continued. "I should be allowed to see David to provide legal guidance."

"Why did he not write to *me*?" Cassandra's voice was barely more than a whisper.

"Perhaps he didn't wish to alarm you?" Hayes suggested.

"Idiot!" Cassandra yelled, so loud they all flinched in surprise. "He didn't think I'd be worried when he never returned?"

"Hush," Helen entreated her sister. "Go and lie down, dearest. I'll relate everything you need to know." She knelt in front of Cassandra and took her hands.

Cassandra raised her chin. "I could never!"

Helen bit her lip. "Will you go to him now?" she asked her uncle.

"Yes, immediately." Hayes stood to go. "And I'll be back as soon as I've seen him."

Cassandra's hand shot out and grabbed his. "Please, Uncle—this must be a mistake. You must sort everything out and bring him back to me. David would never . . . ."

"I'll do everything I can," Hayes assured her, patting her hand.

Hayes departed, Westing following close behind, leaving

the room swathed in silence a few moments.

Helen turned to her sister. "Cassandra, *please* lie down. You look as if you are about to faint. Remember the baby."

Cassandra cradled her stomach with her hands. "All right."

"Wait here while I see to my sister," Helen ordered Nathaniel. Her tone made him nervous. He would have much to answer for. How had he allowed David to get involved in the whole business?

He paced up and down the room, mind unable to settle on any particular thought. The sight of David's prized Chippendale chair made him cringe. Hopefully David would soon return to enjoy it.

With a jolt, he remembered they hadn't retrieved Winthrop's pistol from the dock. He hoped no one would find it.

Helen interrupted his reverie. "Tell me what happened."

Nathaniel related the experience of the previous night. "Winthrop was still alive when we put him in that carriage.

"But you said David struck him with a lantern?" Helen breathed. "Oh, how could he?"

"Winthrop was about to shoot me," Nathaniel admitted. "It was my fault."

"You shouldn't have allowed him to come!" Helen only voiced what Nathaniel already felt.

"I know," he said, massaging his temples.

"How did Winthrop even know you would be there?"

Nathaniel hesitated. "He said—he said a lady told him."

Helen took a step back. "How many ladies have you taken into your confidence?"

Did she think he was calling on many other ladies? How little she knew him! "Only you," he replied stiffly.

Helen gasped. "I never told him any such thing!"

"I should go," Nathaniel suggested. Helen made no reply. Nathaniel bowed. "Please let me know if you hear something."

He walked past the City Tavern, wincing at the memory of meeting David there. He'd betrayed the man completely. Should he step forward and confess the whole scheme to the magistrate? If he did that, he would forfeit all his business and property.

Helen was right to blame him. David urged him not to bring in the tea, to try standing with the Sons of Liberty, and he hadn't listened. David was the only friend he had, and he'd ruined the man's life.

Nathaniel would make this right somehow. He'd go to the jail as soon as possible and offer to take David's place. He could say *he'd* struck Winthrop. He had to do whatever it took to free David.

Cassandra wasn't able to remain in bed long. She alternated between pacing and resting on the drawing room couch when she grew tired.

"Oh, when will he return?" Her eyes darted to the mantel clock once again.

In vain Helen tried to get her sister to eat or take even a sip of broth. The wait seemed unbearable. Neither sister could focus her mind on any occupation.

At mid-afternoon they heard a knock at the door. Helen sprang up to answer it, but Cassandra pushed past her to fling open the door. Her face fell when she saw that it was only their Aunt and Uncle Hayes, unaccompanied by David.

Cassandra sagged onto the door frame. "He's not free?"

"Come and sit, and I'll tell you all I know."

Helen held Cassandra's hand on the couch while their aunt and uncle sat in chairs across from them.

"I was able to see David," Uncle Josiah began. "His valet is with him now."

Cassandra gasped. "Where is he?"

"He's being held at the Walnut Street jail under order of the governor. It seems last evening he met a friend at the docks and some kind of fight broke out. Winthrop Morley was knocked down and died as a result of the blow."

"What evidence do they have that my husband was involved?" Cassandra demanded.

"It seems Winthrop left a letter to his father to explain where he was going, and the governor set out immediately once he had had a chance to read it. He arrived at the docks just as Winthrop's coach was leaving. When he saw his son's condition, he sent Winthrop's coachman out to round up the men who left him, and David was picked up almost immediately off the street."

Cassandra waved impatiently. "Yes, but how do they know it was David and not his friend who knocked him down?"

"According to Governor Morley there was a public altercation at High Street Market between David and Winthrop a few days ago in which David threatened Winthrop."

Helen blanched. "That's true," she said slowly, "But surely David would never . . . ."

"Then there's the matter that David has confessed to knocking down Winthrop," Uncle Josiah continued.

"No!" Cassandra cried.

"He says it wasn't a killing blow and that Winthrop was threatening his friend with a pistol. The constable found Winthrop's pistol at the dock where this all happened."

"Couldn't it belong to someone else?" Cassandra retorted.

Uncle Josiah shook his head. "It's a dueling pistol engraved with Winthrop's monogram."

"Why was Winthrop trying to fire on anyone?" Helen

demanded.

Uncle Josiah spread his hands. “That part is unclear. Perhaps a continuation of the previous conflict?”

Helen wrinkled her nose. She wondered if she should say something. “I believe I know what it was about,” she began, but Uncle Josiah held up a hand to stop her.

“I’ve a suspicion I also know, but I’d rather not have it confirmed. I intend to represent David before the magistrate and would prefer not to have to prevaricate. David has said only that he met someone there, an act which is not illegal. No evidence whatsoever points to any significance to this meeting. If, for example, it was discovered that smuggling was going on, David would be at risk to lose all his property as well as his liberty.”

“What of—the friend?” Helen knew it was Nathaniel, although her uncle avoided mentioning him specifically.

“David wouldn’t name him so he could prevent him from also being imprisoned.”

“He is willing to die to protect his friend?” Cassandra demanded.

Uncle Josiah leaned across and patted his niece’s hand. “Don’t worry overmuch. There’s not much evidence a murder took place—just an unfortunate accident. I plan to petition the magistrate to dismiss the charges.”

Helen didn’t want to upset her sister, but she had to know how feasible this was. “Winthrop mentioned that his father was very close to the magistrate.”

“That is very true,” Uncle Josiah acknowledged.

Cassandra scoffed. “Surely being the son of the Marquess of Dorset counts for something!”

“Yes, my dear, I suspect it will. Our current magistrate has dreams to return to England before too long and would not want to make an enemy of such a powerful family.”

Cassandra looked down. "Can David return home before the trial by paying a bond of some kind?"

"Unfortunately, bond is prohibited for those charged in a capital murder case. But never fear—I'll do all I can to see this is resolved quickly."

"Uncle—I believe you practice mostly in business and estate matters of the law. Are you sure—are you quite sure that you are familiar with this kind of case?" Cassandra turned her wedding ring around her finger.

"When I first began practicing in the colonies, I took every case I could. It's only been in the last few years that I was able to focus on the more lucrative clients to be found in business and estate law." He smiled to show he hadn't taken offense to her question.

Aunt Anne cut in. "Your uncle is very modest, my dears, but he made quite a name for himself defending all kinds of clients. He still receives letters from all over the New World asking for his legal advice!"

"I'm quite satisfied," Cassandra assured them. "I'm sorry to ask, but I feel as though my heart will burst from worry."

"There's no need to apologize," Aunt Anne assured her. "I would be out of my mind with worry if my husband were in a similar situation. You must try to settle your mind, however—for the baby."

Cassandra placed a hand on her stomach. "I'll try," she whispered.

Aunt Anne turned to Helen. "Did you recall that there was to be a meeting of the society today?"

Helen gasped. "Oh! I quite forgot. I'm sorry, but can you give them my regrets? I . . ." She paused, recalling her disastrous decision of the day prior. She would have to make a clean breast of her misstep to the other members. She should probably even resign as president—maybe even as a member of the society. "Maybe I should try after all, though I hate to leave Cassandra." Her sister seemed barely able to support herself.

"I could offer to stay with her, but if you will take my advice, you will postpone the meeting. Temperance has been made quite prostrate with grief over Winthrop's death, and I fear any confrontation would be harmful to both of you."

"Oh dear," Helen stammered, "I-I'm so sorry. I didn't even think about what she must be going through."

"She'll be all right," Uncle Josiah assured her. "The attachment between them was not great. It only existed in Temperance's mind, I believe."

"It was no less real to her than if it had been a recognized engagement," Aunt Anne chided him gently. "In fact, I must return to her soon. Is there aught we can do for you?"

Helen looked at her sister. "No," she replied. "Thank you for coming."

"Uncle," Cassandra asked as they stood to leave, "when you say you will try to move quickly, what do you mean? Could David return home today?"

"Unfortunately, the magistrate is out of town, but he will return early next week."

"Next week!" Cassandra gasped. "Oh, my poor husband! May I go to him?"

"The jail is no place for a woman of delicate sensibility," he insisted.

"If it is no place for me, then it is no place for him!"

"Remember to calm yourself," Aunt Anne reminded her. "For your baby."

"I'll try."

After their aunt and uncle left, Cassandra couldn't be calm, despite Helen's attempts to soothe her. Eventually, she was able to convince her sister to take some laudanum so she could rest for the baby's sake. She drifted off into an uneasy sleep with Helen by her side.

Helen made her way into the kitchen and choked down some stew before returning to her own room. She couldn't find a focus for her mind. Nothing else seemed quite as important as David being imprisoned.

What of Nathaniel? She'd been very unfair to him earlier. David was a determined man. Nathaniel couldn't prevent David from doing whatever he took into his head. She wished he hadn't accused her of alerting Winthrop to his plans. Didn't he know her better than to know she'd never do that? All she could do now was wait, try to support Cassandra, and pray that David would return soon.

Chapter 13

The jail refused to admit Nathaniel as a visitor until Monday. Early in the morning and with very little ceremony he presented himself to the jailer and was told to enter a large room, outside which were stationed two burly guards.

"Jus' raise a noise when you are finished," one guard told him. Nathaniel nodded curtly, hoping they would not mistake him for an inmate of the facility when it was time to depart. Though if he could take David's place, he would do so in an instant and allow the man to return to his wife.

A few men turned when the heavy door was opened to admit Nathaniel.

The room was large, though it didn't seem spacious filled with at least a dozen men. A few sat in isolation, but the rest sat in a large group playing speculation with an odd assortment of buttons, pebbles, and other small trinkets in place of chips. The foul odor of the room reminded Nathaniel of being trapped below deck with sailors who hadn't bathed in weeks.

When David noticed Nathaniel, he threw down his cards.

"Someone else can deal for a while." Groans and protests came from the men. "Now, now, not forever—I just need a break."

It was shocking to see David in this much disarray; he'd lost his wig, coat, and the buttons off his waistcoat, and he was in need of a shave, though his demeanor was surprisingly jolly.

Nathaniel found he was lost for words. "I'm sorry," he finally managed to say.

David waved a hand. "Come, it wasn't your fault. It was foolish of me to pick a quarrel with Winthrop in such a public space. I put myself squarely in suspicion, although I never thought things would come to this pass."

"I should never have allowed you to—"

David frowned. "I must stop you there. I don't recall seeking your permission, nor do I remember you ever entreating me to involve myself."

"You have a family," Nathaniel protested. "I should have found someone else."

"I imagine I'll still have a family when I emerge from this pit. How is she?" David sounded pained for the first time. "Of course Westing is looking after them, but I'd feel better hearing from you as well."

"I've not seen Cassandra since Saturday, though I've spoken with Josiah Hayes. He says she's keeping herself well."

"Hold on, do you or do you not have romantic designs on my sister-in-law? If you are truly enamored of her, I would hardly expect you to keep away at such a time. If you are not, I must beg you to cease trifling with her affections!" David crossed his arms and glared at Nathaniel.

"I'm quite enamored of her," Nathaniel replied, louder than he intended. Some of the card players leaned over to try and hear their conversation. He lowered his voice. "She doesn't want to see me. She blames me for this." Nathaniel gestured to the jail room. "Besides, you ran me off the last time I came visiting without your express permission."

David made another dismissive motion. "I was young and in love once. I hardly think I could have scared myself off. You cannot expect to win fair lady by acting so indecisively."

"You're still young and in love," Nathaniel couldn't resist pointing out.

David shot him an anguished look. "Yes, I am. Which is why I'm asking you to personally visit my wife and sister at this time and ensure they are well."

"I will," Nathaniel agreed quickly. He would do what David asked even if Helen treated him like Beelzebub himself. "But wouldn't you rather me stay here in your place?" He lowered his voice to the merest whisper. "I'll say I'm the one who struck Winthrop, and you can go home."

"You must be joking!" David scoffed. "I've kept your name out on purpose—no sense in you getting thrown in here. Besides, you're a little late. Westing already tried to take my place. He brought a bottle of my finest spirits to try to bribe the guard. I soon sent him packing and gave him a round scolding for trying to dispose of my goods that way."

"Are you certain you don't wish me to intercede?" Nathaniel wasn't worried about himself. He just wanted to make amends.

"Of course not! I know Morley is furious, but I fully depend on the magistrate to let me go free. He's one of those toad-eaters who is always on the lookout for ways to ingratiate himself with great men." He sniffed and examined his fingernails as if to demonstrate that he did not have a care in the world.

Nathaniel marveled that David could manage to look so disreputable and aristocratic at the same time.

"Say nothing," David advised. "Bide your time. Perhaps

attend a meeting of the Sons of Liberty."

Nathaniel began to protest but stopped himself. He might have been able to avert all this by taking David's advice in the first place. "I'll consider it," he finally said.

"And if you want my advice, you should refuse to take any responsibility for this whole thing when you speak to Helen. No matter what she says, *refuse*. Eventually she'll be forced to share your views."

Nathaniel furrowed his eyebrows. This seemed like remarkably bad advice. He ran a hand through his hair and voiced a thought that hadn't been far from his mind the last three days. "I can't believe Winthrop is dead."

"I'd no idea I struck him that hard. I feel terrible."

Nathaniel could scarcely believe it himself. "Do you need anything?"

"A hot bath, clean linens, and a shave are all I desire, but I fear they'll have to wait a little longer. Josiah tells me the magistrate still has not returned yet." David smiled wryly.

"Ho there, your lordship!" one of the men called. "We aren't gettin' any younger!"

"Ah, my retinue," David said with a wink. "Thank you for coming. Please give my wife my regards."

Nathaniel was able to leave as easily as he entered, though he fancied he was the recipient of many suspicious glares. The jail was enormous, built to replace the overcrowded facility on High Street. It seemed the more the city grew, the more the crime did as well.

He shivered a little. It would snow again later. A seaman could always judge the weather. He wished it were as easy for him to know what to do next.

He knew it was probably selfish to think of Helen at this time, but he could hardly stop himself. Was there any chance she could forgive him for leading David into this situation?

And David had just encouraged him to visit her. David might not blame him, but Helen might. There was no way Nathaniel would follow David's advice and try and browbeat her into changing her mind.

He should have given more thought to David's suggestion that he stand with the Sons of Liberty. Perhaps they would prevail in not allowing the *Polly* to unload and the governor would be forced to allow smuggled tea back into the market. Nathaniel would give anything to have David free and Helen speaking to him again—even giving the Sons of Liberty a chance.

What could he do to get David home? Nathaniel had no clout with the magistrate, and David already had an excellent lawyer. If only he could recoup some of David's financial losses. Nathaniel determined to go back to work immediately to figure out how the *Good King George* could bring the most profit. He'd write Cassandra a note explaining how David fared and then visit the women when he had better news.

Helen felt terrible watching Cassandra pace around the apartment, but there was nothing she could do to ease her sister's pain. They'd spent the rest of the day Saturday and all of Sunday in exactly the same way.

She didn't really want to think about the society as a distraction. She'd ruined all their plans. If she'd only listened when Jane told her not to confront Mrs. Morris! Jane would probably never speak to her again.

No, she reminded herself, Jane was too charitable for that. Jane would speak to her out of Christian goodness, even if she privately despised Helen for being so obstinate. Her cousins also would be unable to shun her completely, though they might wish she'd never come to the colonies. Eugenia might be prevailed upon to forgive her. She tried to imagine life with Eugenia as her only friend.

If Helen could only get the rest of the money. She'd still have to explain what she'd done, and the other ladies would likely want her to step down, but at least she would not have to be ashamed of having left poor Mary in an untenable situation.

How could she get the money? The tarts weren't selling quite as well as they had initially. Their friends and family had already purchased several slices, and workers had stopped venturing out as much for food ever since the season's heavy snowfall began. Helen also knew for a fact that there were no gooseberries to be had in the city—perhaps in even the entire colony.

She could write a letter to all the members and confess all, but this seemed a very cowardly thing to do rather than facing them in person. Rather like Nathaniel sending a letter explaining he'd seen David and not coming in person to tell them.

Nathaniel. She didn't wish to think of him at all. How dare he accuse her of conspiring with Winthrop? She'd loathed the man and would not have laid bare any plans to him.

You told Cassandra where David went in the garden, and Winthrop overheard. The thought thudded into her mind, try as she might to tell herself Winthrop must have found out by some other means. David had told her not to tell anyone, and she'd done it anyway, so certain that Cassandra must know.

Could Nathaniel ever forgive her? How much money had he lost in the whole business? It seemed unlikely he would still want to court her after this, if he had ever planned to.

Helen was entirely wretched. She'd been the cause of all this misery, both ruining Mary's chances and landing David in prison. Not only did she need to confess her mistakes to the other ladies of the society, she needed to tell Cassandra she was responsible for putting David in prison. She fell to her knees and prayed that God would help her.

Chapter 14

Nathaniel spent Monday finishing plans for the *Good King George* and gathering the courage to visit the Beaufort home. He'd written, but David had asked him to go in person. When he finally set out on Tuesday, he discovered dense crowds had packed the streets around the Pennsylvania State House, making it difficult to get through to the apartment. As he edged through the crowd, he picked up phrases from conversations around him.

"'Tis a mockery of honest men!"

"We'll not stand for it this time."

"Boston will not fail us! She and New York will stand with us!"

The *Polly* must have docked, he realized. Someone handed Nathaniel a broadside issued by "The Committee for Tarring and Feathering," warning that the captain of the *Polly* should expect swift retribution if he tried to unload his cargo in the city.

Nathaniel shouldered his way almost to the steps of the State House.

"Carter!" someone yelled.

Nathaniel turned around to see Humphrey Goodwin.

"How goes it? Come to see Captain Ayres off?"

"What's going on in there?" Nathaniel pointed at the State House.

"They're voting on resolutions as to how to respond. The *Polly* just docked this morning, but they say Captain Ayres is too afraid to step onto dry land. Ah, have you met Phineas Brand and Sebastian Linch? They're in your line of work."

Nathaniel bowed to the merchants. "We've met."

"'Tis about time we run those tyrants out of the city," Brand said. "I've paid a king's ransom to hold my cargo in a warehouse in Chester."

Linch nodded. "Aye, I sent mine to Virginia and had to sell it as a loss."

They all looked to Nathaniel. "I had to dump mine," he admitted, glancing at Goodwin, who didn't seem to have made the connection that Nathaniel was speaking of cargo he'd invested in.

Brand shook his head. "Some of us were saying we should start a private insurance scheme amongst ourselves. We would each pay a small amount and could make claims against a general fund the next time King George decides to try and put us out of business."

"Lloyd's of London is the place to go for insurance," Goodwin interjected, sounding as proud of the establishment as if it were his own.

Nathaniel blinked at the man's idiocy. "Lloyd's doesn't insure smuggled goods."

Linch cut his eyes towards Goodwin, then turned to Nathaniel. "We're meeting to talk of this at City Tavern later, if you want to join us."

Nathaniel felt a refusal on the tip of his tongue. He didn't often trust other people to make decisions that could affect his business. Still, if he'd been able to insure the cargo, he wouldn't have worried about smuggling it and David would not be in prison.

"I thank you," he said finally. "I should be very happy to join you."

The doors to the state house opened, and a group of men hurried out.

"We've passed the resolutions!" Dr. Benjamin Rush declared. A cry of approval rose up. "Follow me to the docks, and we'll send the *Polly* on her way!"

Slowly the enormous crowd trickled towards the docks. Nathaniel tried in vain to work his way outside the crowd, but it was futile, and he found himself swept along with them.

He saw a man perched in a tree counting people as they passed and scribbling furiously in a notebook. The man met Nathaniel's eyes. "This may be the largest group of people ever assembled in the colonies," he explained. "We are witnessing history. I intend to write about it in my newspaper."

Nathaniel bowed and continued. He wasn't entirely sure the man was correct. Why would history care about this? He just wanted to be able to run his business and, perhaps, if he was lucky, meet a woman who would be willing to throw her lot in with him. If he was very lucky, that woman would be Helen.

He'd never contemplated marriage with any woman before. Would it take another few decades to find someone else he so desperately wanted to spend his life with, or was it possible she would consider forgiving him? Perhaps her heart would be softened if David made it out of prison.

By the time Nathaniel arrived at the dock, Captain Ayres had already been confronted and agreed to leave. Another cheer sprang up among the crowd, and some people started singing a hymn. A little child in front of him waved a flag that had Benjamin Franklin's old "Join-or-Die" cartoon painted on it. Maybe history *would* remember this, judging by the number of people who seemed to find the event meaningful.

Nathaniel made plans to meet the other merchants at City Tavern later in the evening and tried again to make his way to the Beaufort home. The streets were still so crowded that he spent half an hour trying to get down one street. He'd have to try again the next day.

He was unsure if he'd go along with the insurance scheme, but he would hear the other men out. Then tomorrow he would speak to Helen, though he did not plan to take David's advice and speak sternly to her. He knew he had to convey to her what she meant to him, but the thought left his stomach in knots. He had no experience declaring love. In business he preferred the direct approach, and he would have to see if that worked best with ladies as well.

They'd rescheduled the Saturday meeting of the society for Wednesday, and the mood was very different from the first time Helen had presided. Cassandra elected not to attend in the event David was released from jail, Temperance still refused to leave her room, and Jane seemed troubled. Though she wished she could mend things with Temperance and help Jane with whatever concerned her, Helen was relieved Cassandra hadn't accompanied her. She'd had an errand to complete before the meeting, and she wasn't sure if Cassandra would support it.

Euphemia was the only one at the meeting in high spirits,

unable to stop speaking of the events at the State House. "My father was there, did I mention? I begged him and begged him, but I could not prevail upon him to take me, though I found out later that my own maid did attend, for she was out at the market that day to purchase a new pair of stockings for me."

Helen let her continue, hoping to prevent the inevitable moment where the society discovered her failures.

"Is that a new cap, dear?" Aunt Anne asked, passing Helen a cup of tea during a lull in Euphemia's commentary. "I don't think I've ever seen you wear that one before."

Helen reached a hand up and patted the cap absent-mindedly. "Oh—yes."

Finally, even Euphemia ran out of things to say. Helen stood reluctantly. "I call this meeting to order." Patience had a quill poised to record the minutes. "I've something to report regarding our mission," Helen managed to say. Jane smiled encouragingly. Helen cringed and looked away, knowing Jane would have every right to hate her when she admitted the truth.

"I made a grave error. I confronted the woman who holds the indenture we meant to purchase, despite receiving advice not to. She insists we pay her forty pounds for the indenture." Helen paused. "I plan to resign as president of this society."

A stunned silence followed this admission. "As it stands, we have thirty-five pounds," Helen continued. "I'll do anything you think best to find the remainder of the funds. In fact—" She reached up and pulled off her cap. "I've already sold my hair to a wigmaker. He said it was particularly fine and offered me eight pounds for it." Her voice trembled a little at the last.

Euphemia gasped. "Oh, Helen! You are so brave! You quite inspire me."

"Helen." Aunt Anne came forward and hugged her. "How

good you are."

"No," Helen wailed, "I'm not good. I insisted everything be the way I wanted and caused all kinds of trouble. I told everyone we had to sell tarts when gingerbread would have been much easier. I injured Constance by forcing her to go to that horrible fish market. I confronted Mrs. Morris after Jane told me it would be a mistake." Listing her mistakes brought a surprising feeling of relief.

Jane stepped forward and placed a hand on Helen's arm. "I cannot say she would have said anything different to me."

Dabbing at her tears with a handkerchief, Helen turned to Jane. "Mrs. Morris said she would throw your family out of their home if we bothered them further."

Jane scoffed. "Her husband will do no such thing. He doesn't take her advice in these matters."

Helen turned back to Aunt Anne, who was rubbing small circles on her shoulder. "I also upset Temperance by telling her about Winthrop. I thought it would be better for her to know the truth. I should have considered that I might not know best."

"My dear, you did right in telling Temperance of his true nature. In time she'll accept that he wasn't the man she believed he was. Now, perhaps you should know it is forbidden to sell the indenture of a young person at a price over twenty-five pounds."

"What?" Helen said, startled.

"It's the law," Patience explained. "To prevent exploitation."

Euphemia gasped. "You didn't have to sell your hair after all!"

Helen shook her head. The society might not need the money her hair supplied, but she'd needed to feel she was contributing something to make up for her mistakes.

"Perhaps your uncle should have a little talk with this woman?" Aunt Anne suggested.

"She doesn't have to sell the contract," Helen dithered.

"I think perhaps a prominent lawyer with money in hand could convince her of the wisdom of selling it, especially as she could be sued in the court herself if the girl can prove she was mistreated."

"Oh" was all Helen could say.

"I could not bear for you to step down as president," Euphemia declared.

"I don't know . . . ." Helen hadn't dared to hope they would still want her to lead.

"Let's put it to a vote," Patience suggested. "All in favor of retaining Helen in the office of president?" Helen held her breath.

Everyone raised a hand.

"The 'ayes' have it!" Patience declared.

Helen was so overcome with their trust in her that she had to sit and weep into a handkerchief. "Well," she said finally, wiping her eyes, "We have a little more money than we need. Are there any ideas for what we should do?"

Jane raised a hand. "I suggest we continue our operation and begin purchasing the contracts of young women at the indenture market as they arrive in Philadelphia. We could find them paid employment instead."

Helen laughed a little. "I suggest one amendment." Everyone watched her expectantly. "No more gooseberries." The motion was passed unanimously.

Helen returned home a little more cheerfully than when she'd left. Aunt Anne assured the society that Uncle Josiah would take care of the matter of the indenture as soon as possible and said they could offer Mary a position as a maid in their own household.

Her friends' acceptance made her hopeful that perhaps Nathaniel might be able to forgive her also, although he'd lost far more than twenty pounds from her interference. It might take time, but once he'd recovered his losses, maybe he would be able to see past all this. Now they just needed David to return home.

Chapter 15

Cassandra paced in the drawing room when Helen arrived. She'd convinced her sister to bathe and change her shift, but Cassandra insisted on wearing David's wrapper.

"Is there any news?" she asked as soon as Helen entered.

Helen squeezed Cassandra's hands. "Uncle wasn't at home."

"It's been five days since I last saw my husband! I can't wait any longer. I must go to him." Cassandra turned toward the doorway.

"Wait!" Helen laid a hand on her sister's arm. "They don't even allow women in the jail; Uncle Josiah told us."

"They'll not be able to stop me. I must see him! Uncle's reports are not enough—I know he would lie to me if he thought it was for my own good."

"Westing reported David is in good spirits," Helen countered.

Her sister scoffed. "Westing would certainly lie to me on David's order."

"Nathaniel has also seen him and assures us David is well." Helen snatched the letter off a little table and thrust it at Cassandra.

Cassandra swatted the proffered letter away. "Perhaps the reason he wrote instead of coming to tell me is that David isn't well and Nathaniel's a terrible liar."

Helen bit her lip. She had to tell Cassandra the truth. "The reason he didn't come is that he blames me for Winthrop's interference at the docks."

Cassandra turned slowly to look at Helen. "What?"

Helen swallowed. "Winthrop overheard me in the garden. David asked me not to tell you about the smuggling, but I did anyway. If I'd done as David asked, Winthrop would not have known to go to the docks."

Cassandra sank onto the couch where she'd spent so many hours during the last few days. "What have you done?" she cried, then buried her face in her hands.

Helen fell to her knees at her sister's feet and placed her hands on Cassandra's knees. "I'm so terribly sorry. I know this is my fault. I'll do anything to make it right."

"No, it isn't your fault," Cassandra sobbed. "This is all David's fault. Why did he not tell me he was involved in the scheme? I feel I can no longer trust him."

"David loves you very much," Helen assured her. "He wants the very best for you. He invested in Nathaniel's latest venture because he wants to buy a bigger house for you and the baby."

"What? I never knew that either."

"I'm sure David just didn't want you to worry."

Cassandra sniffed. "He did a very poor job of that."

"If you tell him you don't want him to keep secrets from you, he'll listen. Do you recall the pineapple he procured last winter after you mentioned the Harrisons had one? The man doesn't deny you anything!"

"That's true."

"I wish I could find a husband who loves me as much as David loves you," Helen said wistfully. "Though perhaps not as devoted to his wardrobe and with a great deal more sense."

Cassandra laid her hand atop Helen's. "Is it possible you've already found him?"

Helen knew she meant Nathaniel. "He'll never wish to speak to me again."

"I should be very surprised to find that was true. He might be angry, but a man in love will overlook much greater faults."

"In love?" Helen repeated. "I think you are mistaken."

"Perhaps."

The sound of the door opening made them both jump.

"David?" Cassandra flew to the door.

Helen followed close behind her. David was indeed standing in the front entryway, arms wrapped around Cassandra, who was sobbing.

"I thought I lost you!" she cried.

"Never," David assured her, bringing a hand to Cassandra's face and gazing into her eyes.

Love really did overlook a multitude of sins, Helen realized. David hadn't looked this terrible after he recovered from a mild case of smallpox a few years before, and he could certainly stand to take a long bath.

Wrinkling her nose, she started to move towards her room and give the couple privacy. "Glad to see you back," she called. They didn't appear to notice her.

Helen sat on her bed and wondered how to apologize to Nathaniel. Perhaps he would stop by to welcome David home. She could try to seek him out, though it really didn't do for a lady to visit a man in his home. She had only done so in a dire emergency. Did this also count as an emergency? She grabbed her cloak and walked towards the door.

David and Cassandra were sitting next to each other on the couch. Helen was careful not to enter the room all the way so as to avoid the smell.

"Are you going out?" Cassandra called from the couch.

"There's something I must do."

David looked at her sharply. "Helen—you know it wasn't Nathaniel's fault I was arrested."

Helen pursed her lips and stared at David. "Of course I do."

"And you should not blame him—" David continued, as if he'd not yet registered what she said. "Oh. Well, don't punish him too much."

"You mustn't let him get away with no punishment," Cassandra added, gently poking David in the ribs. "He must be made to suffer just enough."

"Just enough. I see."

"You'll always have a home here," David said, just as she turned to leave. "I want you to know that. You're always welcome to live with Cassie and me."

"Yes," Cassandra agreed. "I should like to have you live as near to me as possible, including right here if that is what you wish."

"It will save us hundreds of pounds on hiring a nursemaid over the years," David added.

Helen grinned. "Thank you for letting me know how much I'm worth." She made her way downstairs and out into the cold.

Nathaniel's heart pounded as he approached Helen's street. He wasn't sure exactly what words to use, but he knew it would be cowardly to wait any longer before facing her. Of course, she might refuse to see him at all, but he had to try.

He was just reaching for the latch on the main door to the law office when it swung open to reveal Helen.

"Oh!" She seemed surprised to see him.

Nathaniel gaped at her. "I—you—I—"

"Are you here to see David? He's only just returned."

Nathaniel deliberated and decided to be honest. "I'm very glad to hear David is home, but I didn't come to see him," he admitted.

"Oh. Oh! Well then, I would offer you to come up, but the drawing room is occupied and the air is rather close." She scrunched her nose in memory of a bad odor.

Nathaniel seized his courage once more. "Would you walk with me?"

"I should love to."

Helen smiled up at him, and a weight lifted off his soul. "Is David all right?" he remembered to ask.

"He needs a bath, but he's in one piece," Helen assured him.

"What happened to release him?"

"Do you know, I forgot to ask? I presume Uncle Josiah got the magistrate to waive the charges. I didn't wish to interrupt his reunion with my sister."

Nathaniel tried to think of a way to use this topic to turn the conversation as he intended. "Could you ever forgive me?" he blurted out. It was a good thing he wasn't so awkward in business dealings.

"I'm afraid it is I who must beg *your* forgiveness." She explained what happened the night Winthrop died. "I can't believe I was so unthinking."

Nathaniel shrugged. "You didn't know Winthrop would hear."

"I should have done as David asked."

He stopped walking in the middle of the street and turned to her. "You can't expect your decisions to be right all the time."

"I don't expect them to be always wrong, either, as they have been lately." She gripped her cloak.

"I believe 'always' overstates the case. You managed to increase your initial business investment at an enormous rate."

"I did that with much assistance and some luck," she protested.

"That's the case for most of us, I believe. I've just learned the value of relying on others and could have avoided much misery if I'd discovered it sooner. In fact, I feel *I* must apologize for leading David so dangerously astray."

Helen scoffed. "You mustn't apologize for that. David is foolish enough to lead himself astray without your assistance! I don't blame you in the least."

Nathaniel felt a stab of hope. "I don't blame you for Winthrop's interference. Winthrop didn't have to come to the dock or brandish a pistol at me."

Helen returned his smile.

"Perhaps you could explain something?" Nathaniel suggested after a moment. "I'm very ignorant of these matters. How does a man ask a woman if he can court her?" He could tell, even in the dim light, that she blushed.

"I'm hardly less ignorant of how these matters are conducted in the colonies, but at Heartcomb, he might just ask her."

"Ah. Another matter then—do you think a woman could be happy being courted by a man who owns only two black coats?"

Helen laughed, and his head swum with excitement. "After living with David, it would be a refreshing—oh." She sounded distressed. She *did* mind. He would be willing to buy another coat if it would make her happy. Perhaps a dark blue?

"There's something you must know before you go on." Helen pulled back her hood.

"Is that a new gown?" Nathaniel asked, confused. She was wearing a red gown he'd seen before; he remembered admiring it.

Helen grabbed the white cap off her head. "Can you not see—my hair is gone?"

Nathaniel reached out a hand and gently ran his fingers through the soft, short curls.

"You'll probably start a new fashion," he said softly.

"You've already admitted you know nothing of such matters," Helen reminded him.

"I know only one thing with certainty."

"And that is?"

He stared into her eyes and wondered if this was the right moment. Seeming to sense his apprehension, Helen slid her hand into his.

"I can't imagine going on in life without your intelligence, your humor, your plans and hard work."

Helen stared at him for a moment. "And all my advice and mismanagement?"

"All of it," Nathaniel said.

"What of my gooseberry tarts?"

"I will expect one every time I visit." He squeezed her hand gently.

"Very well—you may court me." She beamed at him.

Nathaniel felt as warm as if they were strolling on a summer's day. Grinning like a fool, he offered Helen his arm and she slid her own through his.

It was dark now, and most people had disappeared into the warmth of their houses. They passed the City Tavern. Nathaniel thought about suggesting they stop but could not recall seeing any ladies in the coffee room. He had so much more to learn about courtship.

"Will you come up?" Helen asked when they reached her doorstep.

Nathaniel glanced up to the window where he assumed David and Cassandra were watching. It was probably best to do this now—to formally ask David for permission to court Helen, as the rules required. "Yes," he said, following her inside.

Helen started up the stairs, but Nathaniel grabbed at her hand to detain her.

"I've another question." His heart drummed in his chest.

"Can it wait until we go upstairs? It's so dark."

"Is it acceptable for a man to steal a kiss from the woman he is courting?"

"Oh!" Helen breathed. "Yes," she answered decisively. "Very acceptable."

Nathaniel brought one hand to her face and gently kissed her. The kiss felt like air to a man who had not realized he was drowning. He placed his hand on her waist and pulled her closer. Helen stood on tiptoes and gripped the lapels of his coat as they kissed more fervently.

The door at the top of the stairs slammed open, flooding them with light. Both Nathaniel and Helen shielded their eyes.

"What is the meaning of this?" David demanded, taking the stairs two at a time to confront them.

"David," Cassandra called from the top of the stairs. "You're being ridiculous."

"I'm looking after the concerns of my sister," David called back.

"You *are* being ridiculous," Helen admonished him. She stepped away from Nathaniel but kept one hand in his.

"Am I? Do you mind telling me what you're doing down here?"

"David!" Cassandra remonstrated. "I'm certain you don't wish to speak of the many stolen kisses we shared before you married me."

"Do you intend to marry her?" David asked, turning back to the couple.

"David!" Helen protested, mortified. Nathaniel squeezed her hand.

"If she decides we'll suit. I mean to court her properly and give her the chance to decide if she'll take a chance on me."

David sniffed and folded his arms. "Very well—I'll agree to it."

"You're not required to agree to anything," Helen snapped. "I'm of age."

"Not required by the law but by the love I bear you as my sister." Nathaniel was surprised to see tears in David's eyes but realized that David had made a habit of looking out for Helen. "I could not be so lucky as to gain a sister and then treat her carelessly."

Helen began crying as well, and the next thing Nathaniel knew she was hugging David, then Cassandra joined them and pulled him in also. He couldn't recall the last time he'd shed a tear, but he was required to wipe a few away.

"Come on then," David said, motioning for everyone to go upstairs.

"I can't imagine how you'll behave when our daughter has suitors," Cassandra told David.

David grinned. "Not to worry; we'll just have sons."

After a round of congratulations, Cassandra gently reminded David that he really did need a bath. She pulled him out of the room, continuing to argue about their unborn child.

"Are you certain you wish to entangle yourself further with this family?" Helen asked Nathaniel.

"I've never been more certain of anything."

Epilogue

Temperance Hayes looked out over the dancers in her drawing room. This should have been *her* wedding feast.

Not that she begrudged her cousin her new seafaring husband. He was handsome enough, in his way, though clearly David should have spent more time teaching him to dance. At least Captain Carter had allowed David to convince him to wear something other than his stodgy black homespun.

Blue suited Helen better as well.

The couple left the dance floor and joined David and Cassandra. In Temperance's opinion, no woman that great with child should appear in public. She could not imagine humiliating herself like that—even for one of her own sisters.

Temperance watched as someone approached the bride and groom with slices of cake. They shared a look she could not decipher, and then Helen took the first bite of her cake.

She leaned forward when Captain Carter raised a fist to Helen. He pretended to thump her on the back, and her cousin burst out laughing.

Temperance rolled her eyes at such childish behavior.

Winthrop would not have behaved so.

"Enjoying the feast, Temperance?" David asked, suddenly appearing by her side.

"Not really."

She ignored his expression of mild surprise. "Would you care to dance, then?"

"Dance with your wife."

"I have been, but she's tired now and asked me to make sure her cousins were engaged."

Temperance sucked in a breath. Thanks to him, she never would be.

"Shall I ask again?"

Temperance glared at him for three long seconds as the piece came to an end and the dancers applauded the musicians. In the brief space of silence between dances, she raised her voice to be heard. "You murdered Winthrop Morley."

The silence stretched out as it seemed half the room turned to them.

David didn't look away from her, though surely he was aware of the gazes upon them. Somehow, he kept his expression as indifferent and aristocratic as ever. "An 'I don't mean to dance tonight' would have sufficed."

After a moment, he nodded to the musicians, who struck up a minuet. Slowly, the dancers took to the floor, and attention turned away from them.

David stepped closer to Temperance, turning his back on the dance floor and the closest would-be eavesdroppers. Now his voice did carry an edge. "I'll thank you not to ruin your cousin's wedding feast."

"Oh? You ruined mine."

"I would be heartily surprised if Winthrop intended to marry you."

Temperance glowered at him. She could march right upstairs and fetch the letters in Winthrop's hand to the contrary. He'd only been dead two months, and everyone else was dancing as if on his grave.

"I'll remind you the magistrate ruled it was clearly self-defense, not murder," David continued. "I never intended—"

"The magistrate trying curry favor with you and your father? That one?"

Clearly her cousin-in-law's temper was wearing thin. "He had a pistol, Temperance. I wonder which of your cousins' husbands you would have preferred to have died that night."

"Better you than him, Lord David."

She hadn't used his courtesy title in years, and judging by his flinch, her words had hit their mark.

"Apparently you haven't noticed," Temperance began, turning to fully face him, "but smuggling is illegal."

"And punishable by instant death? At the hand of the governor's son?"

"According to you two."

Lord David answered with only a single syllable laugh, as if that fact were a mere inconvenience. She supposed it was, when one was rich and noble.

"Get out of my house," Temperance muttered.

He forced on a smile. "I'm hosting this feast."

"Well, I cannot stand to be in the presence of a murderer a moment longer." She stalked from the room.

"Have some cake!" Lord David called after her, as if their conversation had been nothing more than typical party fare.

The feast occupied the whole of the dining room as well, so Temperance marched right out the front door to the porch.

It took all of two minutes to wish she'd had a better plan. A January night in Philadelphia was hardly the place for a fine gown. She had been too angry to pause for a cloak.

She began pacing, rubbing her arms. How long did she

mean to stay out here? Surely Lord and Lady David would be among the last to leave.

She should go back inside and straight upstairs, but Lord David would certainly see her.

She would never forgive him for what he'd done. Never.

Temperance turned back to cross toward the door again when she spotted a man approaching. She tried to gauge how quickly she could make it to the door, in the event this man bore some ill will.

He turned at their walk, and Temperance decided she'd never make the door. She shrank back into the shadows, hoping he wouldn't notice her.

At the steps, the man kicked snow off his shoes. He was almost to the door when he glanced in her direction—and then quickly looked back. "Temperance? Is that you?"

She peered through the shadows at him. "Step into the light?"

He backed up a few paces to the light from the windows.

"Owen Randolph?" Her voice shook with the cold. She'd hardly seen him since they were children. What was he doing here?

"How do you do?"

"Cold."

"Oh, ah." Owen glanced around, then quickly shrugged out of his great coat. "Here."

She allowed him to wrap the coat around her shoulders. She pulled its warmth tight around herself. "What are you doing here?"

"Oh, your father and your . . . cousin? He said I could come. David?"

She scowled. "He's only married to my cousin."

"I see."

Temperance tried mightily but couldn't conjure a reason why Owen Randolph might have wrangled an invitation from either of those people. "How did they come to invite you?"

"Ah, at the office. They said I should come?"

Naturally her father would be at his workplace, and Lord David lived in the flat above the law office. But that didn't explain Owen's presence. "And what were you doing there?"

"I'm studying law. From your father?"

Was he asking her? "How long have you done that?"

Owen squinted at her. "Two years."

How had she not known this? And how had Owen managed that? Last she'd heard, he'd been a stable boy.

"Do you mean to go in?" Owen asked.

"No." Her tone brooked no argument.

Owen hesitated. "Perhaps you should, though? Quite cold. That coat won't be enough for long."

Temperance glanced around. "Can you make sure he doesn't see me?"

"Who?"

"Lord David," she practically spat.

"Your cousin?" He quickly added, "In-law?"

"Yes."

Owen was clearly mystified, but acquiesced. He opened the door and ushered her in. In one surprisingly deft move, he lifted the coat from her shoulders, used it to conceal her until she was on the stairs, and whirled away.

Temperance paused before she disappeared out of sight. Owen Randolph had grown up?

She put that out of her mind and fled to the bedroom. From the bottom of her drawer, she lifted the false bottom and extracted the thin sheaf of papers.

In the moonlight streaming through the windows, Temperance ignored the sounds of the wedding feast drifting up from below and read each of Winthrop's letters once again.

She could never forgive Lord David.

Dear Reader,

Thank you so much for reading *A Lady to Lead*! I'm excited to share my first sweet historical romance with you. I hope you'll continue to join us for all romance of the Revolution!

Do you know the best way to thank an author when you enjoy a book? We do love getting notes from happy readers, but even more helpful is leaving a review online on Amazon or Goodreads. Reviews also help writers get advertising spots and spread the word about a book.

Until my next book comes out, I'd like to invite you to join my mailing group! I've got lots of fun bonuses there, including tart recipes, smuggling facts, that corner chair (it's a Chippendale!) and more! Join me here: http://love.didavisauthor.com/newsletter2

Thanks again for reading, and I hope to see you again soon!

Love,

Audrey Glenn

Acknowledgements

Thanks to my family for all the awesome suggestions!

Thank you to Ashlee, Jessica, Amanda, Allison and Sally for helping improve this book.

Thanks to my coconspirator Diana Davis for investing so much of your time and for talking me through it.

About the Author

Audrey Glenn is a voracious reader who has long loved historical romance. She's a big fan of the classics—*Pride and Prejudice*, *Jane Eyre*, *North and South*, to name a few. She loves studying little-known stories of American history and holds a degree in political science. She lives in North Carolina with her husband and kids in a perpetual fixer-upper.